DRAGONSDALE

Riding the Storm

DRAGON

NSDALE

Riding the Storm

SALAMANDA DRAKE

Illustrations by
GILLY MARKLEW

Chicken House

SCHOLASTIC INC./NEW YORK

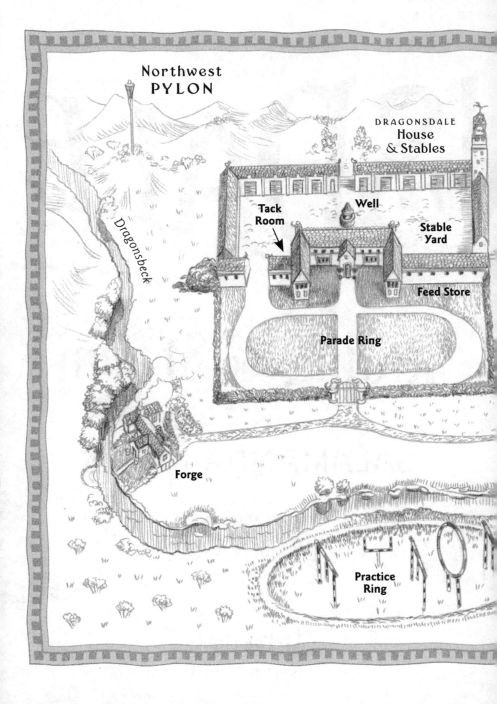

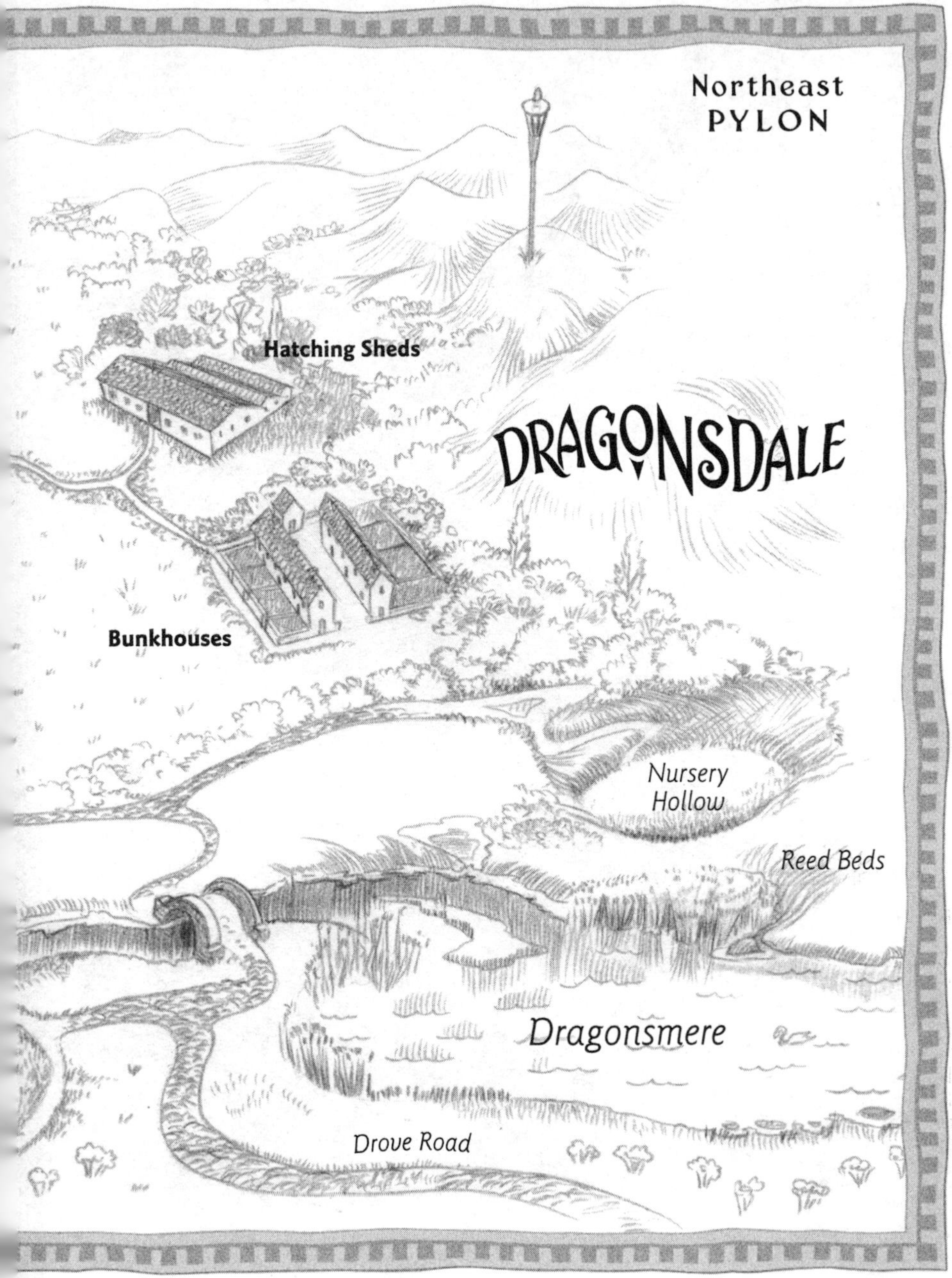

Northeast
PYLON

Hatching Sheds

DRAGONSDALE

Bunkhouses

Nursery
Hollow

Reed Beds

Dragonsmere

Drove Road

The Isles of Bresal

Far out in the ocean, beyond all the shores we know,
hangs a huge bank of mist—the Veil.

The shimmering white curtain of the Veil
hides a wonderful secret.

For beyond the Veil lie the Isles of Bresal—
The Land of the Blessed.

The Isles are home to humans and merfolk, pards
and perytons, howlers and firedogs . . .

. . . and dragons.

For Cathy

Text copyright © 2008 by Salamanda Drake
Interior illustrations copyright © 2008 by Gilly Marklew

All rights reserved. Published by Chicken House, an imprint of Scholastic Inc.,
Publishers since 1920. CHICKEN HOUSE, SCHOLASTIC, and associated logos are
trademarks and/or registered trademarks of Scholastic Inc.
www.scholastic.com

First published in the United Kingdom in 2008
by Chicken House, 2 Palmer Street, Frome, Somerset BA11 1DS.
www.doublecluck.com

Library of Congress Cataloging-in-Publication Data:

Drake, Salamanda.
Riding the storm / by Salamanda Drake ; illustrations by Gilly Marklew. ~ 1st American ed.
p. cm. ~ (Dragonsdale)
Summary: Breena's determination to secure a position with the guard flight by
qualifying for the Island Championships pits her against her best friend, Cara, and
damages the Trustbond she has with her dragon, Moonflight.

ISBN-13: 978-0-439-87174-7 • ISBN-10: 0-439-87174-3

[1. Dragons–Fiction. 2. Competition (Psychology)–Fiction. 3.
Jealousy–Fiction. 4. Fantasy.] I. Marklew, Gilly, ill. II. Title.
PZ7.D78297Dra 2007
[Fic]–dc22
2007035323

10 9 8 7 6 5 4 3 2 1   08 09 10 11 12

Printed in the U.S.A.   23
First American edition, June 2008

The text type was set in Goudy Old Style.
The display type was set in Blackfriar.
Book design by Leyah Jensen

CONTENTS

WIND AND WAVE

"Congested lungs, barking cough, swollen throat, and more soot than a blocked chimney." Alberich Dragonleech finished his examination of Moonflight and stood up. "It's coker, all right. She needs peace and quiet," he went on sternly. "A dose three times a day of my special syrup—my own mixture, mark you, not that quack concoction Mistress Hildebrand sets such store by." He made a disapproving face, and continued, "No meat."

Moonflight gave him a plaintive look and coughed alarmingly.

"And, it need scarcely be said, no flying!" Alberich gave Breena a hard stare, as if suspecting that the minute his back was turned she would instantly saddle Moony and willfully fly her ailing dragon into a state of collapse.

"Yes, Master Alberich," said Breena.

"Well, I'm away to the showing at Wyvernwood. Will I see you there?"

Breena bit her lip and shook her head.

"No, I suppose not. Fare you well—and look after your dragon." Alberich nodded and stalked out of the stable into the cobbled yard with his characteristic heronlike gait. Breena followed him to the door, and stood watching as he mounted a waiting dragon that was almost as lean and rangy as its rider. He strapped himself into the saddle and flicked the hand reins. The dragon unfurled its great wings. As it took off, the skirts of Alberich's leather greatcoat streamed out behind him, flapping as if to assist the dragon's flight. By the time the dragonleech and his mount had risen above the homely stone bulk of Dragonsdale House, it was already difficult to tell where dragon ended and rider began.

Breena returned to the stable, knelt down, and stroked the knobbled ridge above Moonflight's left eye. Moony looked a very woebegone dragon this morning. Her eyes were rheumy and her nose was running. She shifted listlessly on her pumice sleeping platform and snuffled.

"Oh, Moony," said Breena sadly, "what am I going to do with you?"

Cara stuck her head through the open top door of the stable. "How's the patient?"

"Still coughing like a nanny goat," replied Breena. Moonflight gave a hacking cough by way of confirmation. A wisp of smoke drifted from her nostrils.

"Would she like a nice haunch of peryton?"

Breena shook her head. "She's not allowed meat. Alberich said."

"Oh, well—she can have this instead." Cara slipped into the stall and rummaged in a pocket of her flying jacket. She brought out an apple and offered it to Moony, who looked offended and buried her nose under her tail.

"Moony! Manners!" Breena gave her friend an apologetic look.

"Don't worry," said Cara. "I'm always miserable when I've got a sore throat, and look how short my throat is compared to Moony's."

Breena sighed. "Poor old girl."

"Poor old you. You've had such rotten luck this season—too sick to fly at Wingover, and now that you're well, Moonflight's come down with a nasty dose of coker. It's just not fair."

Breena sighed. "Well, worse things happen at sea. Anyway, shouldn't you be heading to Wyvernwood for the showing? You'll want to give Skydancer plenty of time to rest before the Clear Flight competition. Isn't it time you were off?"

"That's why I'm here," said Cara briskly. "You're coming with me."

"Oh, Cara, I'd love to, but I can't. I have to stay here with Moony. . . ."

"Moony just wants to sleep—she doesn't want you fussing around like an old hen."

"But I've got to dose her with coker syrup."

"Bran can do that." Cara nodded to the stable door, through which Dragonsdale's head lad could be heard sending the stable hands about their duties. "He's dosed more sick dragons than Gerda's cooked hot dinners. Anyway, I've never been to Wyvernwood before—you wouldn't want me to get lost, would you?"

"But . . ."

"No more arguments! You haven't been out since Moony fell sick. You'll be coming down with coker yourself next. Everyone's going. Da went across yesterday, Wony left with Mistress Hildebrand first thing this morning, and Drane's riding over on one of the baggage dragons. I've got your flying gear just outside and Sky's saddled and waiting to go."

"You seem to have thought of everything," said Breena ruefully. Then she laughed. "All right! I'd hate to miss the second showing in a row, even if I'm not flying in the competition. And you're right—I can't bear to hear Moony coughing away. I'm a terrible nurse. Just let me have a word with Bran and we'll be off."

Skydancer flew along the gorge of the Tumblewater, above the jumble of rocks that rose like blackened teeth from the raging torrent. The dragon banked from wing tip to wing tip as he followed the winding course of the river, his mighty wings sweeping aside glistening curtains of spray and leaving swirling contrails of vapor in their wake.

Breena, riding in the pillion seat of the tandem saddle, tore off her helmet—in defiance of all safety rules—and peered over Cara's shoulder, her dark hair streaming out behind her. Laughing, she closed her eyes against the sting of the spray and opened her mouth to feel the cool droplets of water on her tongue. "We're getting soaked!"

"Doesn't matter," Cara called back. "We'll dry off soon enough." But she pulled back on the hand reins. "Up we go, Sky!" Skydancer warbled in response and obediently climbed away from the foaming water. Reaching the rim of the chasm, he soared up into a blue sky dotted with fleecy white clouds and turned left to fly low over the dark, sinister pools and wiry grasses of Clonmoor.

"Head more to the south," called Breena, rebuckling her chin strap. "We'll reach the coast at Spindrift Cove."

Cara nodded good-humoredly and did as she was bid. She loved riding Sky, even over this dull landscape, but the coast sounded more promising. She had hardly ever flown over the sea—most of Dragonsdale's training flights took place over the moors or the rolling farmland of the Walds—but she did know that the southwest coast of Seahaven boasted some of the most spectacular scenery in the whole of the Isles of Bresal. It would make a nice change.

Sky flew higher. Before long, there was a glint of silver in the distance, which broadened into a ribbon, then a sheet—and then a vast expanse of shining blue water, stretching to the horizon.

Breena pointed down. "Spindrift Cove!"

They skimmed over granite cliffs and a beach of yellow-white sand where white-tipped waves broke lazily on the shore. "It looks wonderful!" cried Cara. "And Sky loves the sea, don't you, boy?" She reached forward and rubbed at the dragon's long neck. Skydancer gave an affirmative warble. "I wish we had time to stop and look around."

"Maybe another day. I'd love to bring Moony over here when she's better. It feels funny to be flying without her." Breena patted Skydancer's flank. "No offense, Sky." Then she gripped Cara's arm and pointed out to sea. "Look over there! What are those shapes in the water?"

Cara flew Skydancer in the direction of Breena's pointing finger. Soon she, too, could see the dark shapes swimming effortlessly below the waves.

"Oh, look, Cara, they're dolphins." A number of the dark shapes leapt from the water. "No—porpoises."

Cara sighed. "Is that all?"

"Is that all! Since when do you see porpoises every day of the week?"

"Sorry. It's just—I thought it might be merfolk."

"Oh, *merfolk*, is it?" Breena's voice was amused. "You and your stories. You'd be lucky—merfolk don't like being seen. In any case, they mostly live around Merfolk Bay."

Cara nodded, disappointed. She'd loved tales about the merfolk since she was small, and had always wanted to see one. But the people of the sea were shy, and seemed to have little time for humans. *Ah well*, she thought, *maybe someday . . .*

"Let's go, Sky." Cara twitched the reins. "We don't want to be late for the showing." Skydancer swooped low, hooting a farewell to the leaping porpoises, and headed for the shore.

They flew along the coastline. Before long, the sands of Spindrift Cove gave way to towering cliffs. Seabirds, roosting on their rocky ledges, took to the air; they passed and wheeled behind them, calling raucous insults. Cara reveled in the crisp, clean air and the glorious landscape. Above the black-and-gray cliffs lay grassy meadows dotted with the yellow of gorse and the many hues of wildflowers; below them, the tireless, pounding waves crashed against the rocks, sending up white plumes as fine as smoke.

After a while, Breena tapped Cara on the shoulder. "Time to turn inland. Not far now."

Cara was sorry that their journey was nearing its end. Flying with Sky, she felt more alive than she ever did on the ground: Her mind was more alert, her body more perfectly balanced, her senses more finely tuned. Everything about their flight was magical—the sun on her face, the rush of wind all around them, the powerful beats of Skydancer's wings, the shimmering of his scales. And the Trustbond between dragon and rider, intangible but as strong as steel, bound them together more closely than ties of blood or friendship, in ways that a nonrider could never understand.

"We're here!"

Breena's exuberant cry broke Cara's reverie. Moments later they were surrounded by flights of small, two-legged dragonlike creatures that erupted from the trees as Skydancer soared above them.

"Wyverns!" cried Cara.

Breena laughed. "What did you expect around Wyvernwood?"

Easing back with her right hand and foot reins, Cara urged Skydancer into a victory roll out of sheer elation.

The dragon flexed his great wings in response and Cara laughed as the landscape and clouds seemed to spin around her.

"Whoooa!" Breena's grip on Cara's flying jacket tightened. "Give me a bit of warning if you're going to do something like that!"

"Sorry—couldn't resist it!" Cara glanced down. "Look, there's Drane!" She side-slipped to lose height so they could fly alongside a baggage dragon lumbering along at treetop level. The dragon hooted with displeasure and gave Skydancer a sour look, as if to say, "Youngsters today, throwing themselves all over the sky!" Her rider grinned and waved at Cara and Breena. Cara waved back. "Look, Drane! There it is! Wyvernwood!"

The gawky stable hand riding pillion on the baggage dragon shook his head. "I can't see it!"

Breena raised herself in the saddle and cupped a hand around her mouth. "Open your eyes, then, you half-witted hatchling!"

"Not until we're down!" Drane wailed. "I hate dragons . . . I hate heights . . . I hate riding . . . I hate life. . . ."

Cara laughed at his litany of complaints and pulled on the hand reins. Sky banked sharply and settled into a glide.

Breena leaned forward. "There's a good turnout!" she shouted into Cara's ear.

She was right. The sky seemed suddenly filled with dragons. Although Wyvernwood was the southernmost of the five dragon-training stables on Seahaven, and farthest from the island capital of South Landing, there was clearly no lack of visitors for its annual showing. Dragons and their riders were flying in from every corner of the island to watch and compete.

Cara felt Skydancer's excitement mounting at the presence of so many unfamiliar dragons. "Steady, boy." She looked down as they flew over the buildings of Wyvernwood. "It's very different from Dragonsdale, isn't it? The house and stables are separate, not all together like they are at home."

"And look at their guard tower. It has to be tall so that they can see over the trees." Breena pointed to a high platform set on a wooden openwork structure, more like a pylon than a tower, from which the Wyvernwood lookouts could watch for visiting dragons (welcome), emergency beacons summoning the guard flight (less welcome), and marauding predators from the wild moors and hills (not welcome at all).

As they flew toward the tower, a rash of brightly colored signals broke out on the flagstaff at its top. Cara read them carefully; they instructed her to wait for permission to land. Obediently, she made Skydancer waggle his wings in acknowledgment, then banked to the right to join the dozen or so dragons wheeling above the forest, waiting for the ground crew to call them.

"I hope they don't keep us waiting long. Oh, look at that!" Breena's voice took on a scandalized tone as a newcomer, flying from the northeast, was waved straight in. Cara stared at the immaculately dressed rider in the powder-blue riding habit, and her hands tightened on the reins.

"Hortense!"

WYVERNWOOD

Sky bugled a warning and Cara patted her dragon's neck to calm him. Hortense's brief ownership of Skydancer last year had done nothing to make the dragon well-disposed toward her.

Breena snorted. "Unbelievable! Why can't she wait her turn like everyone else? You'd think she owns the place."

"She does," Cara pointed out reasonably. "At least, her da does. You can't expect the High Lord's daughter to hang around up here with the rest of us riffraff. Anyway, she does it to annoy people."

"You're right about that," said Breena with feeling. "She's the biggest troublemaker in the whole of Bresal."

For the next few minutes, Cara and Breena swapped unflattering remarks about Hortense as they waited their turn to land. Far below them, bustling crowds of spectators scuttled among the gaily colored tents, as small and busy as foraging ants, while children and dogs raced here and there, yapping, tumbling, and getting in the way. In the picket lines between the tents and the arena, dragons that had arrived earlier were being fed, watered, and groomed.

Cara cast an appraising eye over the show arena. "It looks smaller than ours."

"It is. Some of the turns are very tight."

"No problem for you, Sky. You like tight turns, don't you?" The dragon craned his neck to give his rider an adoring look and a warble of agreement, and Cara laughed.

One by one, the dragons and their riders were called in to land in a large clearing between the arena and the forest. Some riders wore the green of Dragonsdale, while others were dressed in the colors of rival stables: the scarlet of Clapperclaw, the blue of Wingover, or the brown of Drakelodge. A few wore the parti-colored jackets of private owners.

"There's Hortense's da." Cara and Breena watched as Lord Torin's calash came in to land on a runway that had been set aside especially for the flying chariots.

"Look at him!" Breena was dismissive. "Dressed up to the nines, one hand keeping his hat on, and see how he's clinging to the handrail! You'd think he'd never flown before." Lord Torin's calash swung gracefully in to land, its skids gouging parallel grooves in the lush grass as the dragons pulling it came down running, losing speed steadily as the chariot came to rest.

Eventually Cara was given the signal to land. They glided in, and Skydancer, for all his size and weight, landed as gently as thistledown. Cara took off her helmet and slipped from the saddle.

A young stable hand took Sky's reins. His face was creased in an impudent grin. "Morning, Miss Cara."

Cara felt ridiculously pleased at having been recognized. "How do you know who I am?"

"I was at the Island Championships last Leaf-fall. That was some ride you did—you should've won. I missed the Wingover showing last month, but everyone says you hung out the opposition and left 'em to dry."

Cara flushed with pride. "I had a good day."

"With a dragon like this, you don't need a good day." The stable hand patted Sky's muzzle, admiring the golden blaze on his forehead. "First time I've been this close to a Goldenbrow. He's a beauty!"

Breena swung down to alight beside Cara. "He is that. And he has a good rider. They'll be winning the Intermediate Clear for the second time in a row later on. You'll see." She took Skydancer's reins. "Come on, I'll show you where to go."

Breena led the way between the lines of wattle enclosures. Riders and grooms paused in their work and watched, whispering to each other, as the mercurial redheaded girl who had caused such a ruckus at last year's championships and her graceful, raven-haired friend passed by, totally unconscious of the stir they were creating.

"Here we are." Breena helped Cara lead Sky into his stall and settle him down.

Drane poked his tousled head around the edge of the enclosure. He was still looking worried, as he usually did, but at least he had his eyes open now. "Hello."

Cara raised an eyebrow at him. "Hello, Drane. You survived, then?"

Drane massaged his backside with both hands. "Just. I ache all over. Did I ever mention how much I hate flying?"

"Not more than three or four times a day," said Cara.

"What you two see in riding dragons I shall never understand. The noise! The wind! The swaying! Dangerous, uncomfortable beasts." Skydancer gave Drane a reproachful look and hooted. "Present company excepted, of course," Drane added hastily.

Cara shook her head. "Have you just come along here to rub your bottom at us and moan? Or did you want something?"

"Oh, yes." Drane's brow furrowed with the effort of remembering his message. "The Dragonmaster says if you've remembered to bring his you-know-whats, can you take them to him straightaway." In a low voice, he added, "What are his you-know-whats?"

Cara laughed. "Never you mind." She rummaged in Sky's saddlebags and brought out something that she hid behind her back, away from Drane's prying eyes. "Breena, could you start getting Sky ready, please? This'll only take a minute."

Cara found her father making stilted conversation with Lord Torin. Relations between the High Lord of Seahaven and the Master of Dragonsdale had been frosty since Torin had sold Skydancer back to Huw. The Dragonmaster had given Torin far more for Sky than Torin had originally paid, but the High Lord still felt that, in some way he couldn't quite work out, he'd lost on the deal. Shortly afterward he had moved Hortense from Dragonsdale to the rival stables at Clapperclaw.

Torin's portly figure was arranged in a pose of aristocratic self-importance. His tone of voice was more appropriate for chiding a manservant who had run his bathwater too hot than for speaking to the Master of Dragonsdale. "Must say, Dragonmaster," he was braying as Cara arrived, "'stonishin' the difference in m'daughter's flyin' since she left you, what? Whuff! Movin' to Clapperclaw's been the makin' of her—she's comin' on in leaps and bounds. Leaps and bounds!"

Cara had a mental picture of Hortense desperately clinging to a dragon that was bouncing all over the place like a demented lamb, and stifled a giggle.

Spotting her, Lord Torin gave a snort and a couple of explosive whuffs before turning on his heel and waddling away. Cara was not a popular person in Torin's book, especially now that she was riding Skydancer, the dragon that Hortense had famously failed to tame.

"Ah, Cara." Huw gave his daughter a bleak smile. "Did you bring my . . . um . . . ?"

"Here they are, Da." Cara slipped her father's spectacles into his tunic pocket, taking care that no one else noticed the transaction. The Dragonmaster was very self-conscious about needing glasses. He wore them only in his office, or when, as now, he was judging at a showing and would need to check notes and lists.

"Thank you." Huw patted his pocket.

"Are you judging the Clear Flight competition?"

Huw nodded. "Intermediate and Senior—and the Senior Aerobatics."

"I'll see you in the ring, then." Cara turned to go.

"Cara." She turned back. "Fly well," said the Dragon-master. He gave her an intense look. "And fly safely."

Cara groaned inwardly. Would her father never forget that her mother had died in a fall from a dragon? Would he never stop being afraid that he would lose Cara in the same way?

No, she thought. *Of course he wouldn't.*

Meekly she said, "Yes, Da."

Cara walked around the show arena, carefully memorizing the obstacles and the order in which she had to fly them. Then she reclaimed her competition saddle from the baggage tent. She arrived back at Skydancer's stall just in time to hear Drane say, in sulky tones, "I was only asking. . . ."

She took in Breena's back, rigid with annoyance, and groaned inwardly. Drane had evidently been tactless again. "Asking what?"

Drane turned to her with relief. "I was only asking why Breena didn't just fly another dragon today, since hers is sick, that's all, and she went all hoity-toity on me."

"You asked her . . . ?" Cara gaped at Drane, unable to believe this latest evidence of the depth of his ignorance about all things draconic. "Drane, you've been at Dragonsdale for almost a year now—haven't you learned anything?"

Drane looked hurt. "Well, I've learned which end of a shovel to hold, and not to tip dragon dung out too quickly because it explodes, and—"

"Yes, very good," said Cara, "and we've told you about the Trustbond, haven't we?"

Drane gave a cautious nod. "Yes."

"Well, all riders have to forge a Trustbond with their own dragons. It's between individuals."

"But people at Dragonsdale fly different dragons," protested Drane. "Hortense flew at least three last year."

"Yes, because she didn't have a proper Trustbond with any of them—that's why she's so useless." Cara took a deep breath; explaining things to Drane always made her head spin. "Within reason, any rider can ride any dragon, as long as all they're doing is flying from one place to another, delivering messages or whatnot. But for anything that needs deeper communication between a dragon and its rider—hunting, guard duty, and especially show flying—you can't just suddenly jump on another dragon and expect it to understand what you want it to do. The Trustbond between dragon and rider is special—unique. Some dragons will only accept one rider—"

"Like you and Sky," said Drane, catching on. "He wouldn't let anyone ride him until you did."

"Exactly! For Breena, competing on another dragon would be like entering a footrace blindfolded and with her legs tied together, even if she could bear to do it . . ." —Breena gave Cara a warning glance—". . . which she couldn't," Cara added hastily. "It would be like two people trying to sing together when they only know one song each and it's not the same song."

"All right, all right, I get it," said Drane. "I'm sorry, Breena, I didn't realize—"

"There you are!" His apology was cut off by the arrival of Mistress Hildebrand, the Chief Riding Instructor of Dragonsdale. She was dressed immaculately as usual, with the riding whip she always carried tucked firmly under her arm.

"Yes, we're here," said Cara. "How's Wony?"

Mistress Hildebrand gave her a quelling look. "I wasn't addressing you, Cara. I generally assume that, whatever their other failings may be, Dragonsdale riders can manage to find their way to a showing on time. Wony is a little tired—it's a long flight for a beginner—but she and her dragon have had a rest and they should be in the ring for the Best Presented competition about now. Anyway, I haven't time to stand here gossiping. It's Drane I want to see." Drane shot to attention. Mistress Hildebrand terrified him.

"The Dragonmaster says you're to join the arena crew."

Drane turned even paler than usual and his mouth hung open. He even forgot his fear of Mistress Hildebrand far enough to voice a feeble protest. "Arena crew? But I might have to climb up the masts—I'm scared of heights!"

"Heights aren't anything to worry about," the Chief Riding Instructor told him callously. "Height never killed anyone—hitting the ground, that's what does it. If you're scared of the ground, we'd better get you up high as soon as possible, hadn't we?"

By the time Drane had worked this out, Mistress Hildebrand was a distant figure, marching purposefully to her next assignment. Drane said nothing, but turned and started to make his way to the arena as if his boots were made of lead.

Cara winked at Breena. "Poor Drane. He can't help putting his foot in his mouth."

"If his mouth wasn't so big, he wouldn't be able to get his foot in it," said Breena. Then she gave Cara an apologetic glance. "Sorry. I'm feeling a bit . . ." She fixed Cara with an intensely unhappy look, and words came pouring out of her in a rush. "It's just that this is the last year I can ever be Junior Champion, I'm going to be too old next year, and I've not even qualified for the Island Championships yet, I've hardly even flown Moony this season, and after this showing, there are only three more to go, and if I don't win the Junior Championship, Galen will never allow me to join the guard flight—"

"Hello, Breena. Hello, Cara."

Both girls whipped around. Hortense was standing at the entrance to the stall. Skydancer rumbled a warning, and Cara automatically reached for his head harness.

In a tight voice, Breena said, "What do you want, Hortense?"

"Oh, I've only just heard that Moonflight is sick. I wanted to tell you I was sorry to hear you wouldn't be riding today. It must be beastly for you. Jolly rotten luck." Hortense gave Breena a winning smile. "I hope she'll be better soon." With a nod, she strolled away.

Skydancer gave a hoot of disgust. Breena groaned. "What a time for her to turn up. Trust me to make a fool of myself in front of Hortense!"

"You weren't making a fool of yourself," said Cara. Then she added wonderingly, "Hortense feeling sorry for somebody else? That's a first."

Breena stared with narrowed eyes at the spot where the High Lord's daughter had stood a moment before. "Yes," she said. "I wonder what she's up to."

RUNAWAYS AND ROSETTES

Breena polished a last spot of grime from Skydancer's gleaming scales and straightened up with a groan. "There!" she said, rubbing her back. "If he doesn't win Best Presented after all that effort, I'll eat this brush."

"Ah—didn't I say?" Cara's tone was apologetic. "I haven't entered him in Best Presented."

Breena gave her a jaundiced look. "Then why have I been shining up his mucky hide for the past hour?"

"He still needed grooming," said Cara, "even if he's only entered for the Clear Flight competition. You know how important appearances are in the arena."

"I think *you* need grooming." Breena advanced on Cara with a hard-bristled brush in her hands and a glint in her eyes. Cara backed away, laughing.

"Mercy! I didn't enter him for Best Presented because it's on at the same time as the Beginners' Obedience Test and I wanted to support Wony. You know how much better she's flying—she could have a chance of winning a rosette today."

"Oh, well, in that case . . ." Breena dropped the brush. "You still need grooming, though. You really do. Hurry off and change into your show jacket, and we'll try and do something with that hair of yours." She eyed Cara's wild tresses and shook her head. "You're even harder to make presentable than Skydancer."

By the time Cara was dressed in her prized show jacket, inherited from her mother, and looked as scrubbed and gleaming as her dragon, the novices were being called into the ring. "Now, you behave yourself while we're away," she told Skydancer. The dragon gave a discontented rumble. "Oh, you big softy!"

Cara stroked his eye ridge. "We won't be gone long, and you'll be able

to see us—we'll only be over there."

Skydancer was still not happy about being left alone in a strange place. He hooted and swung his head away.

"I can stay with him," offered Breena.

Cara laughed. "You don't have to. He's just being a big sulky baby. Aren't you?" She rubbed the dragon's neck. "You'll be fine." She made sure that Sky was firmly tethered to the picket; left to his own devices, he would probably try to follow her. Then she and Breena set off to catch up on Wony's progress.

The path to the Novice Ring was lined with stalls. Some of these were selling roast potatoes, hot chestnuts, and other snacks ("Flame-grilled sausages with hot sauce—they give you the breath of a dragon!"). Others were peddling all manner of goods associated with dragon-riding—clothing, tack, tools and brushes, patent oils and quack medicines, toy dragons on sticks, and dragon kites.

Behind the stalls, a spirited game of skittles was taking place, with successful pitches greeted by cheers and unsuccessful ones with groans and laughter. Along the pathway, some of Wyvernwood's more enterprising stable hands were selling baskets of steaming dung to gardeners ("Guaranteed fresh—straight from the dragon this morning!"). Chattering crowds sauntered here and there, examining the goods for sale, greeting acquaintances, or simply enjoying the fine weather and the company.

"We won! We won!" A familiar voice rang out from the crowd. Wony appeared, leading a swaggering Bumble and brandishing a large gold rosette. "First place for Best Presented!" Wony's smile was as wide as a dragon's wingspan. "My first-ever gold!"

Cara gave a cry of delight. "Well done! That's your reward for all those hours of hard work grooming Bumble. I told you it would be worth it."

Wony gave her rosette an uncertain look. "I just hope I can do as well in the flying competition."

"You're getting better all the time," Cara reassured her. "And the more you practice, the more you'll improve. You know what Mistress Hildebrand says about that: 'Riders are made, not born.'"

"But you'd never ridden a dragon until a few months ago," Wony protested, "and then you flew the only clear round at the Island Championships, and won at Wingover in your first showing. You don't need to practice—you're a natural."

"She's got you there, Cara." Breena's smile was slightly lopsided.

Cara flushed with embarrassment. "We all need to practice . . . ," she said.

"Some of us more than others," sighed Wony.

A deep bass voice cut off any further discussion. "Will competitors for the Beginners' Obedience Test please make their way to the ring."

"That's me," said Wony. "I'd better warm up Bumble. Can you look after this for me, please?" She handed Breena the gold rosette. The older girl stared at it wistfully.

Cara recognized her friend's mood. In all the years that her father had forbidden her to fly, Cara had wondered many times whether she would ever ride a dragon, let alone win a rosette. "Don't worry," she told Breena. "You'll have one of those, when Moony's fit again—and it won't be for Best Presented, it'll be for Intermediate Clear."

"But I'd have to beat you to do that," said Breena.

. For a moment, Cara was speechless. This had quite simply never occurred to her. Amid the joy of riding Sky, developing their Trustbond, being—at last—part of the world she had always longed to join, there had been no room in her thoughts for more practical considerations. Breena was her friend—it had never even crossed her mind that she was now also her rival.

Cara tried to break the sudden tension with a laugh. "I'd not have won at Wingover if you'd been riding."

"Wouldn't you, so?" said Breena quietly. "I wonder."

They faced each other in silence for a moment. Then Cara turned back to Wony. "Come on, let's get you sorted. Time to win gold number two!"

The Fun Ring was an area of meadowland marked out by ropes slung between whitewashed wooden posts. Young dragons and their riders were already warming up, practicing the simple maneuvers that would demonstrate to the judges that they had mastered the fundamentals of dragon flying. Wony led Bumble to a mounting block next to the ring and, with help from Breena and Cara, hauled herself onto her dragon's back and settled into the wood-and-leather saddle.

Breena gave Bumble a pat on his flank. "May the winds blow kindly . . ."

". . . and the sun shine upon you." Cara completed the Old Bresalian saying, wishing her friend good luck.

With a pull on the leg reins and a flick of her wrists, Wony urged her dragon forward to begin their warm-up. Bumble had grown a lot over the last half year and looked as if he'd at last found out what his wings were for, though there was still something of the bumblebee about his flying.

"How do you think she'll fare?" whispered Breena.

Cara shrugged. "Obedience Tests aren't like Clear Flights. It depends on how the judges mark the riding. At least with a Clear Flight everyone can see whether you've hit the obstacle or not."

"Less chance for favoritism," agreed Breena. "Thank goodness, or Hortense would win everything!"

Cara laughed. "Come on. Let's go and see what Wony's up against."

The two girls hurried over to the ring. As the early competitors took their dragons through the required elements of walking and jogging, take-off and landing, they cast expert eyes over each performance and made critical comments about the riding skills of Wony's rivals.

"Not enough tempo in that turn."

"Too much shoulder, not enough leg."

"Where's the rhythm?"

Their most critical observations were reserved for a young boy representing Drakelodge and riding a small Finback dragon. The hapless rider had no control of his mount whatsoever. The dragon stood stock-still in the middle of the ring, willfully ignoring its rider's commands and gazing around as if it were saying, "I'm not listening—la la la la . . ." The rider frantically pulled on his leg and hand reins in an attempt to get his mount to move. It was useless; the dragon's reaction was merely to plonk itself on the ground with its forelegs folded across its nose.

In frustration, the boy gave the creature an almighty crack with his whip. Startled, the dragon sprang up and ran at full speed toward the judges' tent, with the boy bouncing out of his saddle and hanging on for dear life. Two of the judges looked up, aghast, then dived beneath the table, scattering notes, rosettes, and trophies all over the place. Only Mistress Hildebrand held her ground. She merely folded her arms and stared defiantly at the dragon as if to say, "I dare you." Just as it seemed that she was about to be squashed flat, the dragon gave a flick of its wings and took off, much to the amusement of the crowd and the relief of the judges.

Despite the boy's attempts to bring the dragon back around, it continued to fly off in a straight line. Its rider's cries for help became fainter as the Finback passed over the slated roof of Wyvernwood and skimmed the trees surrounding the stables. The crowd was in an uproar as a ring marshal was dispatched to chase down the errant dragon and its rider and bring them back.

"Well, at least Wony shouldn't finish last," said Breena. "Not after that display!"

Once the crowd had settled down, the announcer called for the next competitor. "Taking the ring now is Pollenbloom, ridden by Wony of Dragonsdale."

Cara and Breena cheered as Wony urged Bumble into the ring. For the next few minutes the girls rode

every move with her, their hands and legs twitching at imaginary reins, urging Bumble on, pulling him back when needed, and whispering encouragement.

"That's a good tight circle," said Cara.

"Keep your head up," muttered Breena. "Not too fast into the take-off."

They needn't have worried. Bumble's stubby wings flapped twice and he was in the air, flying a figure eight. Three circuits of the ring later, Cara and Breena clapped their approval as Wony brought her dragon in to land. With a final salute to the judges, she exited the ring.

Cara and Breena hurried to the paddock. "Well done!" cried Breena. "That was fantastic, Wony!"

"Was it?" asked Wony uncertainly. "Good enough for a rosette?"

Cara gave a decisive nod. "Definitely."

The few remaining competitors put their dragons through their paces, after which there was a pause while the judges retired to their tent to confer. By the time the competitors were called into the ring for the presentation, Cara and Breena were back among the spectators. Cara gave the judges a distrustful look.

"Mistress Hildebrand will be fair to everyone, and that's got to be good for Wony. Hoyt of Wingover I'm not sure about. But look who's head judge—Adair of Clapperclaw. You know how he hates Dragonsdale. And he's the one holding the rosettes."

UP IN THE WORLD

The Dragonmaster of Clapperclaw was tall, and thin to the point of being skeletal. His eyes, hard and watchful, were set deep in his skull-like face, and he glared at the crowd as though defying it to disagree with his judgments.

"Here are the results of the Novice Competition," he announced. "After some spirited discussion with my fellow judges"—he favored Hildebrand with a hard stare—"I have made my decision. In third place, and winner of the green rosette, is Hilda of Wingover."

There was a smattering of applause as the rosette was handed over. Wony shifted nervously in her saddle.

"And now for second place, and the blue rosette goes to . . ." Adair deliberately paused, creating even more tension both in and outside the ring. ". . . Lelia of Wyvernwood."

A loud cheer went up from the home supporters.

"Wony's going to win gold!" whispered Cara, hardly daring to believe it.

"Maybe . . . ," said Breena guardedly.

"In first place, and winner of the gold rosette in Beginners' Obedience, is . . ." Adair moved purposefully toward Wony and Bumble.

"Yes! Two golds!" Cara laughed out loud.

But her joy was short-lived. Adair veered away from Wony and handed the gold rosette to a young girl dressed in the scarlet of his own stables. "Violet of Clapperclaw!"

Wony gave an involuntary moan and closed her eyes to stop the tears from flooding out. She turned Bumble and filed out of the ring with the others. Breena and Cara met her at the gate to the paddock.

"That was so unfair!" Cara told Wony. "You were robbed."

"What a fix!" Breena was furious. "How does Clapperclaw get away with it? The judges can't know a thing about riding."

"I trust that you are not including me in that observation."

Wony and Cara froze at the sound of Mistress Hildebrand's voice, but Breena was unabashed. "Wony deserved to win a rosette," she told the Chief Riding Instructor fiercely. "You know that as well as we do."

Mistress Hildebrand ignored Breena's outburst and turned to Wony. "For what it is worth, I had you down as a rosette winner, but I'm afraid Dragonmaster Adair marked you down. Master Hoyt also commented that you looked a little tired on some of your moves. But after your long journey here, perhaps that was to be expected."

Wony sighed. "Ah well, maybe I'll have better luck next time."

The Riding Instructor shook her head. "I don't think so."

Wony's face dropped. "Oh, I thought you said—"

"If you will allow me to continue, young Wony—there will not be a next time because I believe you are ready to move up a class. So, no more Obedience Tests. At the next showing it'll be the Beginners' Clear Flight for you! I will see you in the nursery hollow next week for some obstacle training."

Mistress Hildebrand turned her attention to Cara. "Speaking of Clear Flights, hadn't you better be getting ready for the Intermediate Clear? They're off in five minutes. And a word of advice—be careful of the double horizontal. It looks tricky. Don't approach it too fast, and trust your dragon on the turn out. Good riding."

As Mistress Hildebrand marched off, Wony remained quite still, wide-eyed and openmouthed. "Clear Flight, Clear Flight . . ."

Cara's anger had melted away. "Wony, did you hear that? You're going up a class!"

"What a day!" Wony threw her arms around Bumble's long neck and squeezed tightly. The dragon gave a hoot of surprise. "Oh, Bumble, I love you so much!" She gave the dragon another squeeze. "I'm going to find some food for

Bumble, then I'm going to find the cake tent for me! Do you want to come?"

Cara shook her head. "I'd love to, but I need to warm up Sky." She pointed to Wony's gold rosette. "I'm going to see if I can win another one of those."

Cara and Wony, leading Bumble, walked away, laughing and talking a mile a minute. Breena looked down at the rosette in her hands almost as if she were afraid of it.

Then she shook herself and set off to follow her friends.

Cara left Breena and Wony to untack Bumble, and hurried back to Skydancer. The dragon gave a hoot of recognition and flapped his wings in happiness at her return.

"Steady on, silly," said Cara, rubbing at Sky's flank. "I said I wouldn't be long." The dragon draped his long neck over Cara's shoulder and nuzzled his head against her back. "All right, all right. Don't get too excited." She reached for Skydancer's head harness and looked into his eyes. "We're flying for gold, remember—for Dragonsdale, and my ma."

Skydancer gave a reassuring warble, and Cara rested her forehead briefly against the golden blaze on his brow. Very quietly she said, "You're the best dragon in Bresal, and I don't deserve you." Sky shook his head, spread his wings, and bugled.

Cara laughed. "All right, have it your way. Let's show 'em what we can do together."

A bell rang out, signaling the beginning of the Intermediate Clear. Breena joined Cara as she led Skydancer over the cropped grass of the meadow toward the competitors' paddock. "Have you had a look over the obstacles?" She glanced at the nearest mast, and her eyes widened. "Look, there's Drane. What's he doing up there?"

High above the ground, standing on the lower of the two crosspieces and clinging to the mast as though his life depended on it—which, in fact, it did—Drane was wondering the same thing. He'd obeyed Hildebrand's command and reported to the arena ground crew. "I'm Drane, I've been sent to help you." Once the riggers had stopped laughing (Drane wondered what he'd said that was so funny), the largest of them stepped forward.

"Pardon us, lad, just a bit of merriment. Don't be takin' it all personal, like." He held out a leather-gloved hand, which Drane took; it was like being gripped by a padded vise. "I'm Fergus of Wyvernwood, chief rigger." Fergus looked Drane up and down. "Don't want to be appearin' rude, like, but 'ave you actually ever done any riggin' at a showin'?"

Drane had to admit that he'd never done any rigging at a showing, or anywhere else for that matter, an admission that brought a shaking of heads and a winking of eyes.

"Ah well, lad, we all 'ave to start somewhere. An' I reckon you can start up there." He pointed to one of the six tall masts that supported the obstacles for the Clear Flight competition high above the arena.

Drane turned even paler than usual. "Up there . . . ?"

"Oh, yes." Fergus nodded. "You'll be positioned on the crosspiece, on account of you lookin' like a regular squirrelman." More laughter greeted this.

"What's a squirrelman?" asked Drane, already certain that he wasn't going to like the answer.

"Well, Brane . . ."

"Drane," corrected Drane. "My name's Drane."

"Sorry, Brane." There were more suppressed snickers. "When the dragons fly into the poles or 'oops and they drop to the ground, someone's got to pick 'em up and put 'em back into place. That's what us riggers do. But there's different jobs, see. We 'ave the pickers-up — that's them." Fergus nodded toward a group of young stable hands from Wyvernwood. "We call 'em ring-rats, on account of 'em scurryin' and 'urryin' around the ring like rats, pickin' up the poles as quick as you like." Fergus turned to the ring-rats. "'Specially when Miss 'Ortense is flyin', 'ey, lads? I've never seen a rider 'ave more poles 'it the floor! Like apples on a windy Leaf-fall day. You 'ave to watch yer 'eads when she's about!"

Despite his nervousness, even Drane managed a smile at the thought of Hortense's riding.

Fergus continued his explanation. "Then there's the tuggers—that's them beefy-lookin' lot." Drane glanced across at this group, noticing that their arms were as muscled as a dragon's forelegs. "They're in charge of the ropes that 'old up the obstacles. Now, there's different types of ropes. . . ."

"I guessed there might be," said Drane, his head spinning.

"There's the uphaul an' the downhaul—there's an inhaul and an outhaul as well, but you don't need to bother about those. Let's keep it simple, eh?"

"Yes, let's," said Drane faintly.

"Now, the uphaul 'auls up and the downhaul 'auls down—you with me so far?"

"Er . . ."

"So if a pole gets knocked off, the tuggers 'aul up on the uphaul. This is where the squirrelman—that's you—comes in. . . ."

"Oh—do I?"

"Oh, yes." Fergus gave the ground crew an exaggerated wink. "Now, when we've 'auled up on the uphaul, you 'ot-foot it along to the end of the crosspiece." The last traces of color left Drane's face. "An' you attach the uphaul to the downhaul. Then we 'aul down on the downhaul, letting out the uphaul, obviously . . ."

"Obviously . . ." muttered Drane, closing his eyes.

". . . until the end of the uphaul is down. Then we

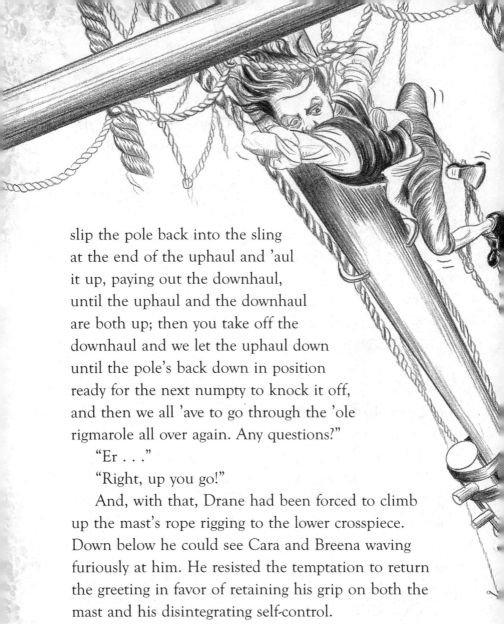

slip the pole back into the sling
at the end of the uphaul and 'aul
it up, paying out the downhaul,
until the uphaul and the downhaul
are both up; then you take off the
downhaul and we let the uphaul down
until the pole's back down in position
ready for the next numpty to knock it off,
and then we all 'ave to go through the 'ole
rigmarole all over again. Any questions?"

"Er . . ."

"Right, up you go!"

And, with that, Drane had been forced to climb
up the mast's rope rigging to the lower crosspiece.
Down below he could see Cara and Breena waving
furiously at him. He resisted the temptation to return
the greeting in favor of retaining his grip on both the
mast and his disintegrating self-control.

Back on the ground, Cara pouted. "Rude thing, not

waving back to us! Ah well, if he wants to have fun climbing up ropes, then that's up to him."

"Boys," said Breena, "always having to be climbing things. If it's not trees, it's ropes." She gazed at the rods hanging between Drane's mast and its neighbor. "Anyway, about these obstacles . . ."

"I took a look at them earlier," said Cara. "The only real problem is the one Mistress Hildebrand mentioned—the double horizontal. It's a steep dive to the second set of rods, but I think Sky can handle it."

"I'm sure he can—" Breena was interrupted as the announcer's voice rang out across the arena.

"Our first rider in the Wyvernwood Showing's Intermediate Clear is the High Lord's daughter, Hortense, representing Clapperclaw and riding Silvercloud." There was a muted response from the crowd sitting in the temporary wooden grandstand as Hortense, riding a female Bearded dragon, flew into the center of the ring and saluted the judges.

"Get the garbage out of the way," observed Breena. "And save the cream until last."

Cara smiled. She'd been drawn to fly last in the competition, which was a mixed blessing. On the one hand, she would know how her fellow competitors had fared. On the other hand, it created its own tension: If a previous rider had flown a clear round, it meant that one mistake from Cara would mean no gold rosette. She gave a shrug. "You never know. Hortense might have become a good rider over the past few weeks."

Breena arched an eyebrow. "And dragons might swim."

GOING FOR
GOLD

The bell rang for Hortense to begin her round.

High above Cara and Breena, Drane crossed his fingers, then suddenly realized he'd taken his hand off the crosspiece and grabbed back at it, clinging on for dear life. He gave an involuntary moan. "Please don't knock down my rods, Hortense. Knock down all the others, but please, not mine . . . oh, no!" Drane realized he was clutching at straws as Hortense turned her dragon too quickly into a set of horizontal rods and clipped the bottom one, sending it crashing to the ground to receive ten penalty points. He glanced earthward to see the ring-rats rushing from their positions to retrieve the fallen rod (while not forgetting to keep a wary eye on Hortense's next maneuver).

On the ground, Breena clicked her tongue. "That's her done for. She'll go to pieces now." Cara nodded in agreement.

On the crosspiece, Drane was thinking the same thing. A second mistake by Hortense and another pole

went scudding to the ground. Just three more obstacles to go and she would be arriving at Drane's mast. He couldn't bear to think about it. "Please take a wrong course," he begged. "Then you'll be disqualified and you won't have to attempt this one." He suddenly brightened. "Or crash—crashing would be good!"

His pleas went unheard, and although two of the three obstacles went tumbling earthward, Hortense turned her dragon and headed for the mast where Drane clung

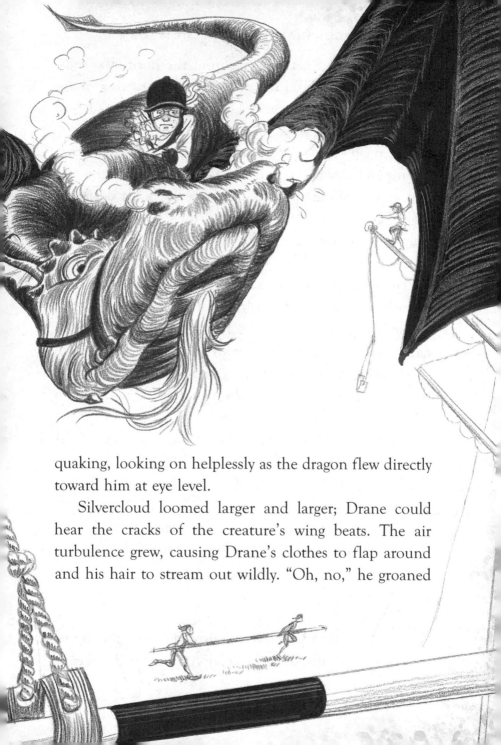

quaking, looking on helplessly as the dragon flew directly
toward him at eye level.

Silvercloud loomed larger and larger; Drane could
hear the cracks of the creature's wing beats. The air
turbulence grew, causing Drane's clothes to flap around
and his hair to stream out wildly. "Oh, no," he groaned

again as Hortense set her dragon at the horizontal rods.

There was a sound like thunder and a roaring of air. Instinctively every muscle in Drane's body tightened, and he scrunched his eyes shut.

Then all was quiet. The maelstrom subsided in an instant and Drane carefully opened an eye. Hortense and Silvercloud had disappeared from view. Hardly daring to look, Drane glanced down at the rods. They were both swaying, but they were still in place! "Yes!" he cried. "Yes! Yerrr . . . no!"

He had spoken too soon. The obstacle continued to rock back and forth on its stout ropes; Hortense had gotten the angle of approach wrong and Silvercloud had clipped one of the rods with her tail.

As if in slow motion, the top rod began to shake loose from its sling. There was a collective drawing in of breath from the crowd as it tipped over.

Drane closed his eyes. "Noooooo!" he cried. But despite his plea, the yellow-banded rod fell, crashing into the bottom one and sending both rods hurtling to the ground, causing the ring-rats to flee for their lives.

Two obstacles later, Hortense's ordeal was over—and so was Drane's. The High Lord's daughter had completed her round with six obstacles down, and scored sixty penalty points.

"Come on!"

Drane looked up. The squirrelman on the upper crosspiece was already halfway along the wooden beam, balancing on top of it like a tightrope walker, as easy and carefree as if he were walking along a garden wall.

Drane was appalled. "I can't do that!"

"There's a hoof rope for them as needs it." The squirrelman grinned down at Drane. "Take the downhaul with you—that line there. Arms over the crosspiece, trotters on the hoof rope—you'll soon get the hang of it."

Drane really, really doubted this, but he unhooked the line the squirrelman had indicated and, holding it between his teeth, lowered himself with infinite care, feeling for the hoof rope, then inching along it with his upper body draped over the crosspiece like a drowning man clinging to a spar.

Guided by the shouts (not unmixed with oaths) from below, Drane reached the end of the crosspiece, located the uphaul, and attached the line he had carried out. Down below, the ring-rats pulled hand over hand, and the rope ran, chattering, through its wooden pulley block as the sling sank to the arena floor. The ring-rats slid the pole back into place, then—carefully keeping pace with the crew of the mast to which the other end of the pole was attached—the tuggers raised the obstacle until it was hanging just below the crosspiece, beside Drane.

Responding to more shouts from below, Drane gingerly reached out with one hand, his head swimming, to detach the downhaul. He forced the line between his chattering teeth and began the long, terrifying creep back to his place of safety beside the mast.

He had barely reached it by the time the next competitor clipped the pole, sending it spinning to the ground once again. Drane closed his eyes.

As the competition continued, Drane was called into action many times; as Mistress Hildebrand had predicted, the double horizontal obstacle to which he was assigned was causing great difficulty for all the riders. No one managed to clear it. Competitors came and went, watched closely by Cara, Breena, and Wony, who had finished rubbing down Bumble and joined her stable companions.

"Not many to go now, and no clears yet," said Wony. "You're going to win gold, Cara."

"There's still Ernestina," warned Breena.

"Yes, there's still Ernestina," agreed Cara. "And she's next. . . ."

Both girls respected Ernestina as a rider, despite the fact that she was based at Clapperclaw and friendly with Hortense. She had a strong Trustbond with her dragon, a dark-scaled Shadowhide called Stormbringer, and was a technically competent and brave competitor. This was borne out by the number of gold rosettes she'd won at showings, and even at the Island Championships, over the past few seasons.

As if to prove Breena's point, Ernestina's riding of Stormbringer was immaculate. The first few obstacles were flown with an ease that made all the riders who had flown before look clumsy and labored. Ernestina was a different class of rider, so when she headed toward the tricky double horizontal, Drane was feeling confident that he wouldn't be called into fixing the obstacle.

He was wrong.

As Ernestina urged her dragon between the parallel rods, Stormbringer's wing just clipped against the side rigging rope, causing the lower pole to topple groundward. The crowd let out a sympathetic "Ahhh!"

"Not again," groaned Drane. "I swear they're all doing it on purpose!"

As Ernestina completed her round, finishing with ten penalty points, Wony jumped up and down in excitement. "There's just Cara to go and no one's clear!"

Breena nodded. "You only have to fly clear, and you've won. Good luck."

Cara said nothing; her face was set with determination. She hardly heard the announcer calling her forward, or the cheers from the crowd as she flew Skydancer into the ring.

"Come on, Sky," she whispered. "We're flying for gold!"

She tugged on the reins, and with an excited hoot, Sky surged forward. They were through the first hoop in an instant, the dragon pulling in his wings tightly in answer to Cara's urging.

A fierce joy flooded through Cara as she guided Sky around the arena. Her communication with her dragon was instinctive: A pull on the hand reins or a flick of the leg, and Sky knew exactly where to go. Trust was everything between them. Dragon and rider moved as one, Cara bending and curving in the saddle in response to Skydancer's every movement, the dragon reacting to every twitch of the reins and every suggestion made by his beloved rider. The rods and poles were not to be feared. Obstacles? No, they were simply guides to their flight. The idea that Sky might hit one was inconceivable.

On his mast, Drane had almost forgotten his terror, captivated as he was by Cara's riding and by the grace of Sky's movement through the air as they threaded the obstacles. Seeing the dragon's flight from up here, for the first time he dimly grasped what it was that drove Cara and Breena, that kept them going through the long hours of unrelenting practice in all weathers, and the frustration that Breena must be feeling, being unable to ride.

Breena watched Cara's round from the paddock, her thoughts in turmoil. She should be up there, flying for Dragonsdale, if only Moony were fit. Poor Moony, how she missed her. She wanted Cara to go clear, of course she did—Cara and Sky flew so well together. Had she and Moony ever flown so well? Could she and Moony ever . . . ? Something seemed to blur Breena's vision. Angrily, she rubbed at her eyes. She noted with astonishment that the back of her hand, when she drew it away, was wet.

No mistakes so far, and now Cara and Sky were heading toward the tricky horizontal. But instead of speeding up to take the obstacle as every other rider had done, Cara reined back, slowing Sky until he was almost hovering, to make sure her line of approach was absolutely right.

The crowd held its breath—very few intermediate riders were capable of displaying such control over their dragon. Few had the confidence, fewer still the nerve. In the judges' tent, Huw nodded and murmured, "Good girl." Mistress Hildebrand raised an eyebrow and made a hurried note on the program sheet.

Cara took the first part of the double in a slow, shallow glide, then she squeezed her knees tightly together, pulled on the foot reins, and urged Sky into a steep dive toward the second part. In a blur of green and gold, Skydancer flashed past Drane and flew between the poles with a handsbreadth to spare.

"Yes!" Drane punched the air in celebration, wobbled perilously, flung his arms around the mast, and clung to it for dear life, his heart hammering against his ribs.

Cara headed for the final two obstacles. "Come on, Sky," she murmured, "hold it together. Nice and easy does it and the gold's ours." She sent Skydancer into a steep dive before leveling out and flashing in and out of the series of tall willow wands sticking up from the ground. *Flick – flack – flick – flack* . . . Sky weaved from wing tip to wing tip in a continuous slalom, his tail missing the wands by a scalesbreadth each time.

Then it was just a few wing beats to the final horizontal. "All right, Sky," urged Cara. "Over to you." And she took all the pressure off the reins, allowing her dragon to judge his own body position and speed.

Sky felt the relaxation of Cara's hands and realized that she was placing her trust in him. With a hoot of excitement, he sped on and shot through the obstacle without displacing a single rod.

"She's done it!" screamed Wony. Breena nodded and smiled, but her eyes were unusually bright and her lower lip trembled. The crowd broke into thunderous applause. They knew they were seeing a rider and dragon who were a cut above the rest.

Cara was ecstatic. She slapped and slapped at Sky's neck as she flew around the arena, waving to the cheering crowd. Even Drane forgot his terror just long enough to give her a big thumbs-up.

There was no need for the judges to confer. A few minutes later, Cara mounted the winner's rostrum to receive her rosette and trophy.

"What a day!" cried Wony, applauding wildly. "Two golds for Dragonsdale!"

Breena gave her a rueful smile.

"Only a couple of people have ever won a gold rosette at every showing during a season," Wony went on. "I bet Cara can do it. She's beaten everyone else twice already!"

"Not everyone," said Breena quietly. "Not yet . . ."

Wony stopped clapping. "Oh—sorry. I didn't mean . . . I was just . . ."

"Never mind." Breena's eyes were still on Cara, who had now left the rostrum only to be surrounded by a crowd of spectators and fellow competitors, all offering congratulations. Breena turned away. "Look," she said, "Drane's coming down. Let's go and see what sort of day he's had."

They joined Drane, who was surrounded by the rest of the ground crew. A grinning Fergus was slapping Drane heartily on the back. "What did I say, lad? What did I say? You're a natural squirrelman!"

"Urgh," said Drane, still quivering.

Fergus motioned to the rest of the crew. "And me an' the lads 'ave decided that 'cause you're such a natural, you're goin' to be promoted."

"Promoted? Me?" Drane could hardly believe his ears.

"Oh, yes, you are goin' up in the world." Fergus pointed skyward. "Next showin' you can go up onto the top crosspiece."

The two Dragonsdale riders just managed to catch Drane before he hit the ground in a dead faint.

ALARM BELLS

Some weeks later, Cara and Breena were sitting at the large bog oak table in the kitchen of Dragonsdale House. Gerda, the roly-poly housekeeper, bustled about, carrying the lunch pots and pans to the sink, where Drane stood, soapsuds up to his elbows, scrubbing the china plates that, minutes before, had been piled high with Gerda's delicious meat-and-gravy pie. The kitchen wyverns, perched on the mantelpiece over the vast range, shuffled their wings and watched him with beady eyes.

Drane reached for another plate from the stack. "Why do I have to do this while you sit there on your backsides, chatting about nothing?" he complained.

"Because we didn't forget to tell Gerda how delicious her special treacle pudding was," replied Cara.

"Now that's a terrible accusation, my girl," said Gerda. "As if I'd let a tiny thing like that influence me." She slammed a large iron pan down on the draining board, making Drane jump. Her eyes narrowed. "And make sure you get all the grease off that!"

"But it was delicious," protested Drane. "All your food is delicious. You're the best cook in the whole of Bresal, you know that. . . ."

"Nice to be told, though," said Gerda. "We all need a bit of praise once in a while. It stops us feeling that we're being taken for granted. Now, less moaning and more scrubbing, or I'll find some more chores for you. The upstairs rooms need a good sweeping and dusting."

As Drane groaned, she winked at the girls.

The kitchen door opened and Mistress Hildebrand stepped in. "Ah, Breena, Cara, I thought I'd find you here. Good afternoon, Gerda."

"And to you, too, Hildebrand. You're a little late for lunch, I'm afraid. Between Galen's guard flight and these greedy boobries, there's not a scrap left."

Mistress Hildebrand shook her head. "No time for that. There's work to be done." The riding instructor turned her attention back to Cara and Breena. "Have you finished all the mucking out and grooming yet?"

"You don't have to ask," said Breena glumly, "you only need to smell us! We built up a real sweat in this hot weather."

"If you've not built up a sweat, you've not done a good job," said Mistress Hildebrand matter-of-factly.

"I must be doing an amazing job," muttered Drane, wiping his brow.

"I'll need your help this afternoon," continued Mistress Hildebrand. "I've got a group of first-timers coming up from the village. The Dragonmaster has gone to South Landing to order supplies from Forrager's Feedstuffs and I need as many riders as I can get to keep an eye on the youngsters."

Both Cara and Breena groaned inwardly. Helping out with first-time riders was a real bind, usually involving dealing with children who wouldn't listen to any form of instruction, and mopping up their tears when they suffered the consequences of not listening. On the plus side, these lessons brought money into the stables and occasionally led to some of the richer parents being persuaded to buy one of Dragonsdale's dragons.

Despite this, Cara really didn't want to be burdened with the chore. She had set her heart on spending some time practicing with Skydancer. "Sorry, Mistress Hildebrand, we'd love to help," she said untruthfully, "but before he left, Da said me and Breena had to check the hatchling sheds and make sure the dragonets were all right."

Drane saw an opportunity to avoid any further housework. "I can do that for you, Cara," he said.

Both Cara and Breena shot Drane a killing stare.

Mistress Hildebrand raised an eyebrow in surprise. "That's very kind of you, Drane—you're a good lad."

"Thank you," said Drane. "It's nice to be told once in a while. It stops me feeling that I'm being taken for granted."

Before Gerda could throw a dishcloth at Drane for his cheekiness, the raucous clanging of the alarm bell sounded from outside.

In an instant, Cara and Breena had thrown back their chairs and followed Mistress Hildebrand out of the kitchen. Hurrying into the stable yard, they glanced up at the watchtower, where the lookout was ringing the large brass bell for all he was worth.

Within seconds, the cobbled yard was a hive of activity. Like all the stables in Bresal, Dragonsdale had a duty to those farms that had paid a tithe to keep them safe from the beasts of the Isles. Firedogs, howlers, and sometimes the even more fearsome pards roamed freely in the hills and moors, and there were even occasional reports of wild dragons attacking isolated farmsteads. When that happened, beacons would be lit and the guard flight would take to the air.

Bellowing to make himself heard above the din of the bell, Galen, Dragonsdale's chief huntsman and leader of the guard flight, commanded his riders to saddle up. "Where's my dragon?" he roared. "Where's Nightrider?" The stable hands fell over themselves to appease the grizzled, sharp-tongued Flight Leader.

Several of the other dragons in the yard, including Skydancer, thrust their heads over their half-open iron stable doors, hooting in excitement at the hubbub. One or two of the younger dragons spat out dribbles of flame.

"What's going on?" Cara asked Tord, one of Galen's wing leaders.

"Missing child," Tord replied briskly. "Farmer's daughter from Scar Ridge. Her pet wyvern flew away and she set off to find it."

Galen counted his flight and shook his head. "Only five of us. Imar and his men are still hunting on Wildernesse, and Mellan's delivering a message to Clapperclaw. We're short of riders for a search." He scowled. "We'll just have

to spread out, keep our eyes peeled, and cover as much ground as possible. There's no time to waste. It's wild country up there."

The other riders nodded grimly. Scar Ridge was on the rocky northern slopes of Mount Cloudhead. Anything could happen to a lost child in such a lonely place.

"I could go with you."

Galen turned to see Breena standing before him.

"Moonflight's fit enough now," she said. "Her coker has cleared up. I could fly out with you. I know the area well enough. I could be another pair of eyes for you. . . ."

"Hmm." Galen scratched at his stubbled chin as he considered Breena's offer.

Cara looked on, her heart in her mouth. She knew how much this mattered to Breena, who wanted desperately to become a rider in the guard flight. Galen had been putting her off for months, telling her that she wasn't ready and had to prove herself by winning the Junior Championship. Breena was convinced that Galen didn't want her in the flight because she was a girl, but she had never dared tell the cross-grained Flight Leader this to his face.

"Breena is a more than competent rider," said Mistress Hildebrand, appearing at Galen's shoulder. "I'm sure she won't let you down."

Breena's eyes lit up at the riding instructor's vote of confidence. Galen made a sour face, but he nodded. "All right, but you fly with me and you don't go off on your own."

Breena gave a squeal of delight. "Yes, Galen! Thank you!"

"Well, what are you waiting for? Saddle up quickly."

Breena raced to Moonflight's stable. Cara followed her. "I'll help you tack up."

Breena was ecstatic. "I'll prove to Galen I'm worth my place! He'll have to let me join then." She flung open the heavy iron door. "Come on, sleepyhead," she told Moonflight. "We're going to fly with the guard flight!"

For the next few minutes, Cara and Breena rushed around, tacking up the excited dragon. Both of them were all fingers and thumbs at the urgency of the task.

"Hurry up!" Galen's impatient voice sounded from the yard. "Don't be all day about it!"

Breena clipped the last rein into place. "Done!" She and Cara led Moonflight out into the yard — and stopped, looking skyward as a beating of wings overhead heralded the arrival of a newcomer.

Mellan, the missing rider from Tord's flight, brought his dragon in to land and waved to Galen. "You can stand down," he called. "I found the girl. She's back home safe and sound."

"You found her?" Galen demanded. "How did you even know she was missing?"

Mellan laughed. "I didn't. Her wyvern found me. I was on my way back from Clapperclaw, and the thing kept flying around my head until I gave in and followed. It led me straight to the girl."

"It sounds as if the beast has a lot more sense than its mistress." Galen turned to the lookout tower and gestured. The alarm ceased. "Stand down, men."

The riders of the guard flight dismounted and began to untack their dragons with the help of the stable hands. Crestfallen, Breena fought back the tears of disappointment that were welling up inside her.

Tentatively Cara patted her friend on the shoulder. "Never mind, Breena. You'll get another chance."

"When?" Breena clenched her fists in frustration. "Galen keeps saying I have to prove myself, but how can I do that if he won't let me fly with him?"

"But he's said he'll consider you for a place if you do well in the Island Championships."

"I've got to qualify for them first."

Cara tutted. "You'll do that. The Drakelodge showing is next month, and Moony's fit again. If you finish in the top three, you'll qualify!"

Breena sighed. "You're right. Sorry, it's just that . . . you know." She rubbed Moonflight on the shoulder. "Sorry for getting you all tacked up for nothing," she said to the dragon.

An idea struck Cara. "Look, Moony's all ready to fly, and helping out with the first-timers won't be much fun. It's such a lovely sunny day—why don't I saddle up Sky and we'll both fly off to the beach? We could go to Spindrift Cove—remember, we saw it on the way to Wingover and said we'd like to go there when we had time? Well, let's go there now. It'll do you good!"

Breena's face lit up. "Do you think we'd get away with it?"

Cara smiled. "No problem. I'll have a word with Gerda, I'm sure she'll make up some story to cover for us. Oh, come on, Breena. It'll be fun!"

Breena made up her mind. "All right! You're on!"

FRIENDS
TOGETHER

"Come on in, Moony. The water's—"

"F-f-freezing!" howled Cara.

"I was going to say 'refreshing.' Try it!" Breena scooped up a double handful of sparkling water and threw it over Cara, who squealed and splashed back in retaliation. Then they both ducked and gasped as Skydancer, flying above them, suddenly folded his wings and belly-flopped into the sea with a crack that echoed around the cliffs, creating waves that threatened to swamp them. Cara and Breena turned their attention to splashing Sky, who gurgled with pleasure, rearing up and using his body and half-furled wings to create a surge of water that bowled both girls off their feet. Moonflight, who had been pacing back and forth along the sandy beach, hooting unhappily, set up an anguished trumpeting.

Cara staggered to her feet. "Not fair!" she cried. "Stop it, you big bully!" Sky snorted happily and flapped his wings to dry them, his sails cracking like gigantic handclaps.

Breena surfaced, coughing and spluttering. "Moony!" she gasped. She waded clumsily through the shallows to throw her arms around her distressed dragon's neck. "I'm all right, see?" Moonflight crooned anxiously.

"We're only playing. Come and join us!" Breena tried to tug Moonflight forward, but the dragon dug her talons into the sand and straightened her forelegs. She looked so like a gigantic dog trying to avoid a bath that Cara, standing waist-deep in the sea, doubled up with laughter.

"Come on, you old silly. It's fun!" Breena went round to the back of Moonflight, set her shoulder against the dragon's haunch, and pushed, with no noticeable effect. "Look at you, great mollycoddle that you are." She gave up, returned to face Moonflight, and planted her fists on her hips. "For shame, a big strong dragon scared of getting a little wet!" Moonflight gave an apologetic hoot, but showed no sign of going any closer to the water.

"Never mind!" Cara called. "Most dragons don't like the sea."

Ignoring Moonflight's piteous warble, Breena waded out to rejoin her friend. "Why is that, d'you suppose? They're happy enough to splash about in the Dragonsmere."

"Well, people do say fire and water don't mix. Maybe it's the waves. I mean, the sea is pretty wild sometimes, isn't it? Perhaps they realize that it's one of the few things in Bresal that's more powerful than dragons are. One minute it's calm, and the next . . ." Cara threw a great splash of water at Breena, hitting her smack in the face. ". . . it's stormy!"

Breena spluttered, "I'll get you for that!"

Laughing, Cara threw herself backward and swam away in an easy backstroke, kicking water at Breena as she waded vengefully in her wake. But suddenly Breena gave a startled cry, threw up her hands—and disappeared beneath the waves.

"Breena!"

Cara was almost deafened as both Moonflight and Skydancer trumpeted with alarm. "Breena!" She flipped over and swam to the spot where the water had closed over her friend. Sky took off with a thunder of wing beats and a cloud of spray and hovered overhead, hooting anxiously.

Breena rose to the surface, head back, spluttering and thrashing at the water with her arms. Cara lunged forward and, just as Breena began to sink again, she slipped behind her and slid her arms beneath Breena's. Locking her fingers behind her friend's neck, she began to tow her to the shore, kicking hard. A few moments later, Cara's kicking heels touched sand, and she released Breena, who staggered to her feet, chest-deep in water.

Sky, who had been hovering overhead nervously, gave a relieved hoot and settled back into the sea. Breena coughed and wiped water from her eyes. "Thanks."

Cara brushed her friend's long dark hair away from her face. "You must have stepped off a sand ledge, into deep water. Are you all right?"

"I'm fine." Breena coughed again. "I'd better see to Moony." She waded toward the shore, where Moonflight, despite her fear, was standing in the shallows, still making pathetic and most undraconic whining noises. As Breena approached, Moonflight stretched out her neck and surveyed her rider anxiously, alternately warbling concerned inquiries and scolding as she would an erring dragonet.

Followed by Sky, Cara waded to the beach. Breena, who was stroking Moonflight's muzzle, turned at her approach. "Thanks again." She gave a shaky laugh. "I'm glad you were close by—and I'm even gladder you can swim!"

Cara gave an embarrassed shrug. "Sky would've saved you if I hadn't." She rubbed her bare arms. "Come on, let's get this salt off us. There's a waterfall over there."

For the next few minutes, Cara and Breena took turns showering under the waterfall, gasping at the coldness of the water, which had begun its journey to the sea as snowmelt from Cloudhead. Skydancer splashed back into the sea and lay in the shallows, his great scaly body rocking gently in the breaking waves. Moonflight retreated up the beach, as far from the sea as possible, and curled up with her nose under her tail, occasionally opening an eye to check that her mistress wasn't getting up to any more aquatic foolishness.

After their showers, Breena and Cara sat together on a rock, letting the sun dry their sodden clothes. Cara rested her chin on her knees and gazed out to sea. "It's so beautiful."

"But sad, too." Breena's voice was somber. "I know of a place where the sea weeps."

"Weeps?" Cara glanced at her friend, startled.

"Yes, a few times every year. It makes a strange moaning noise—like a lament."

"Where does the noise come from?"

"I don't know," admitted Breena. "It just seems to come from the sea itself as it strikes the land. There's a cave there—the fisherfolk call it the Cave of Sighs. It's an eerie sort of place."

Cara looked at the blue water with its lazy, white-crested waves. "It looks so peaceful."

"It isn't always. When a storm comes in, the wind roars like a pard. The waves crash on the rocks as if they want to tear the world apart, and the sea takes poor fisherfolk's boats and drags them down into the dark." Breena shuddered.

"Your da was a fisherman, wasn't he?" said Cara tentatively. She knew that Breena and her family didn't get along.

"Was," said Breena. "He has a stall in the fish market at South Landing now. He wanted me to take over the boat when he retired." She shuddered again. "I told him I preferred dragons. He's hardly spoken to me since."

"But if you grew up with fisherfolk, why did you never learn to swim?"

"Fisherfolk don't," said Breena.

Cara stared at her. "Why not?"

"It's a sort of superstition—they think that if they can't swim, their boat will take care of them, but if they can, one day their boat will sink and they'll have to take care of themselves."

"That doesn't make sense!"

"It's a superstition, of course it doesn't make sense." Breena lay down on the rock and stretched. "In any case, merfolk swim."

"And fisherfolk and merfolk don't get along," said Cara.

Breena laughed. "That's a polite way of putting it! They hate each other. The fisherfolk say the merfolk tear their nets and steal their fish."

"And what do the merfolk say about the fisherfolk?"

"I don't know, I haven't asked them."

"I wish I could meet one of the merfolk," said Cara wistfully. She scanned the sea to the horizon. "I wonder what their lives are like, down there under the sea. Wouldn't it be strange to live where there's no wind or grass?"

"I daresay they have—oh, currents in the water, and seaweed and stuff," said Breena vaguely. "Sometimes I wish I were a mermaid. Then I wouldn't be so scared of the water."

"But if you had a fish tail, you wouldn't be able to ride a dragon," Cara pointed out.

"True." Breena stood up. "Race you to that big rock and back—that'll dry us off nicely."

As Cara and Breena flew back toward Dragonsdale, the sun sank lower in the sky and the barren wastes of Clonmoor rolled below them. The inhospitable landscape was a wilderness of wiry grass, moss-covered boulders, and peat hags interspersed with bracken and clumps of heather. Here and there, clinging stubbornly to the rocky ground, stood brakes and thickets of stunted, arthritic-looking trees, bent eastward by the raging winds that hurtled in from the sea to lash them every winter.

Cara had lapsed into a pleasant daydream in which food, especially Gerda's best crumbly scones with wild raspberry jam and lashings of clotted cream, featured heavily, when a whistle from Breena jerked her out of her reverie. She looked hastily around just as Moonflight flew alongside. Breena reined her dragon back to keep pace with Skydancer and pointed with one gauntleted fist. She mouthed the word "Perytons!"

Cara looked down and saw that Breena was right. A small herd of the winged deer was grazing on the sparse grasses of the moor. Cara watched them, marveling at their beauty and the daintiness with which they stepped between the tussocks of wiry grass.

She turned back to Breena. "So?"

"Let's go hunting!"

Cara was horrified. "Hunting? But we're not trained for hunting, either one of us."

"Oh, come on! What's so hard? We need to work around to the west so that we fly at them out of the sun, then in we go and—*wham!* Roast peryton for supper."

"But why?" blurted Cara. "There's plenty of food in the store at home."

"What of it? The hunters always say the meat tastes twice as good when you've caught it yourself. Anyway, it'll be fun! And just think—if we come back with a peryton we've caught ourselves, won't it be a poke in the eye for that oaf Galen! He'll find it harder to turn me down for a place in the guard flight then."

Cara wasn't at all sure about that. Besides, she had no wish to harm the beautiful winged deer. She would steel herself and take an occasional gory haunch to Sky, because she knew that peryton was his favorite meat, but she always avoided eating it herself if she could. "We should tell the hunters about this herd," she said. "They can come back with a properly organized party, and—"

"And by that time, the herd will have disappeared and they'll never catch them."

"But they're so pretty," said Cara lamely.

"Oh, Cara!" Breena gave a snort of impatience. "If you're going to be such a baby, I'll hunt them myself, so."

"No—I'll come." Cara's heart was beating quickly, and she had a lump in her throat as if she'd swallowed too much cold porridge, but she couldn't abandon her friend.

"Well, come on, then. Wait until I'm in position, then dive into the middle of the herd to scatter them. I'll come in from the west and separate one from the others, then we can hunt it together."

"All right." Cara felt it was very far from all right, but she was committed now. She watched unhappily as Breena peeled away and flew in a wide half circle, losing height, to place herself between the herd and the westering sun. She wondered what had gotten into her cautious, sensible friend. It never occurred to Cara that Breena might feel overshadowed by her own achievements and feel the need to match them in some way.

As Moonflight swung around to begin her run, Cara gave a sharp tug with both leg reins, then eased back on the right. Skydancer obediently banked over and into a near-vertical dive.

Regardless of her misgivings, a fierce grin spread over Cara's face at the sheer exhilaration of speed and power. The wind tugged at her clothing as she and Sky fell, causing the sleeves and skirts of her leather flying jacket to flap wildly. Despite her goggles, her eyes watered, and tears ran down her cheeks, stinging her face as the wind dried them instantly. Her knuckles, knees, and thighs ached with the effort of holding on to the reins and saddle.

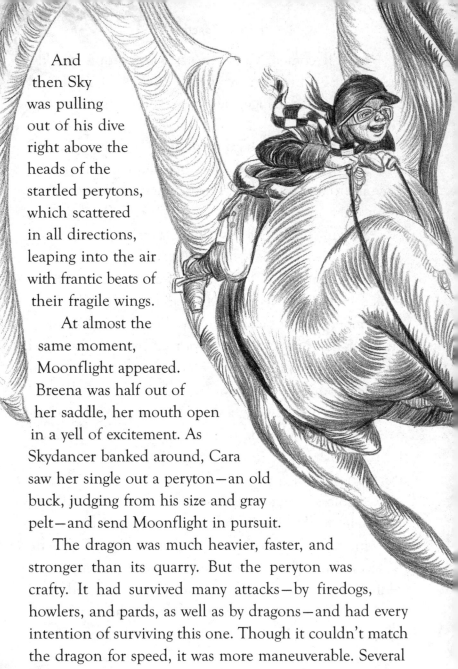

And
then Sky
was pulling
out of his dive
right above the
heads of the
startled perytons,
which scattered
in all directions,
leaping into the air
with frantic beats of
their fragile wings.

At almost the
same moment,
Moonflight appeared.
Breena was half out of
her saddle, her mouth open
in a yell of excitement. As
Skydancer banked around, Cara
saw her single out a peryton—an old
buck, judging from his size and gray
pelt—and send Moonflight in pursuit.

The dragon was much heavier, faster, and
stronger than its quarry. But the peryton was
crafty. It had survived many attacks—by firedogs,
howlers, and pards, as well as by dragons—and had every
intention of surviving this one. Though it couldn't match
the dragon for speed, it was more maneuverable. Several

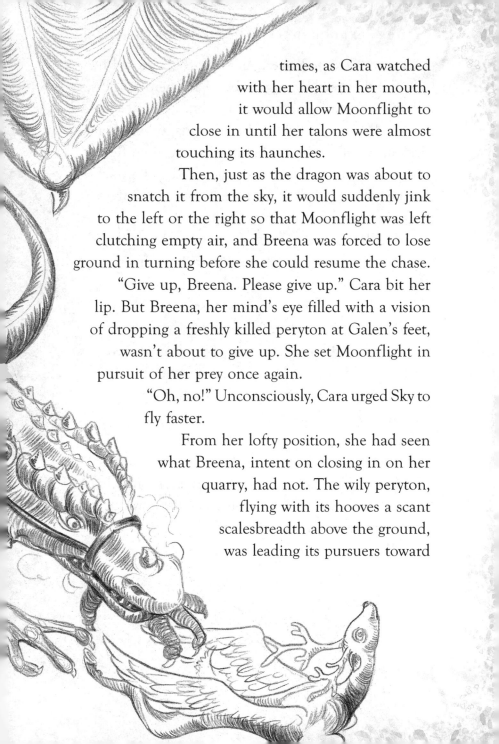

times, as Cara watched
with her heart in her mouth,
it would allow Moonflight to
close in until her talons were almost
touching its haunches.

Then, just as the dragon was about to
snatch it from the sky, it would suddenly jink
to the left or the right so that Moonflight was left
clutching empty air, and Breena was forced to lose
ground in turning before she could resume the chase.

"Give up, Breena. Please give up." Cara bit her
lip. But Breena, her mind's eye filled with a vision
of dropping a freshly killed peryton at Galen's feet,
wasn't about to give up. She set Moonflight in
pursuit of her prey once again.

"Oh, no!" Unconsciously, Cara urged Sky to
fly faster.

From her lofty position, she had seen
what Breena, intent on closing in on her
quarry, had not. The wily peryton,
flying with its hooves a scant
scalesbreadth above the ground,
was leading its pursuers toward

a thicket of stunted trees. As Moonflight closed in, it reached the trees, zigzagging between them at full speed.

Moonflight began to pull up, but as Cara watched, aghast, Breena hauled on the leg reins, urging her dragon to follow. Moonflight hesitated, then flew lower, skimming the ground, and tried to follow the peryton through a gap between two pine trees that was just too narrow.

Needles exploded from the trees as Moonflight's wing tips ripped through their branches. Breena threw her arms up in front of her face as her dragon, legs and wings flailing, lost control and crashed into the midst of the thicket. Moorland birds exploded out of the trees, branches swayed and snapped, and a cloud of leaf mold erupted from the ground as the dragon's body slammed into it. Then all was still.

Cara brought Sky in to land at the edge of the thicket and hurled herself from the saddle. She tore off her helmet and goggles as she raced through a shower of falling pine needles toward the scene of the crash. "Breena!" she cried as she ran. "Breena!"

A BROKEN BOND

The bell in the guard tower pealed out, splitting the still evening air. The sound echoed from the stone walls of Dragonsdale House, clamoring its urgent message into every corner of the stable yard. Three strokes, then a pause, then two more, over and over again.

Galen, who was talking to the other members of his guard wing, swung around and stared skyward. Wony and Drane, working in the stable yard, looked up, startled. "What's happening?" demanded Drane, dropping his broom. "Are we being attacked? Is it firedogs? Howlers? Pards?"

Wony shook her head. "That's not the signal for an attack. It means there's a wounded dragon coming in."

"From the guard flight?"

"Can't be," said Wony in a tight voice. "Galen's wing is back and Imar's has only just gone out. They haven't had time to get into trouble yet."

The Dragonmaster strode out through the kitchen door, shrugging into his tunic as he came. Gerda, a worried look on her round, homely face, bustled behind him, dusting flour from her hands. Alberich Dragonleech, who was treating one of the racing dragons for set-fast, stalked from the stable, a mixture of anticipation and professional detachment on his gaunt face.

The lookout in the tower continued to sound the alarm with one hand. With the other, he pointed to the southwest. Every head in the yard turned to scan the skies in that quarter.

Two dragons were approaching, flying slowly. The first seemed to be carrying two riders. The dragon to the rear was clearly in trouble: Its flight was erratic and labored, and its wing movements were jerky, as though it found the effort of flying painful. As it came nearer, jagged holes and rents were visible in its sails.

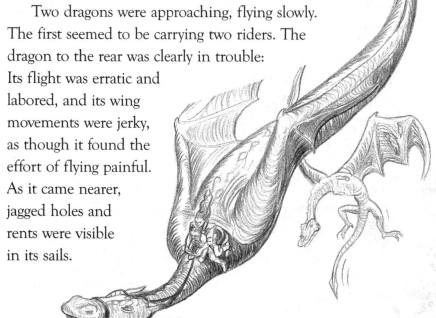

"Clear the yard." Huw's voice was harsh.

Wony's mouth was hanging open. "That's Breena and Cara on Sky . . . and Moonflight's hurt. . . ."

"I said, clear the yard!" The Dragonmaster's sharp command sent Wony and Drane scuttling out of the way. Galen and his wingmen led their dragons into their stalls; grooms pushed curious muzzles back inside stables and closed the top doors. The sight of a wounded dragon was guaranteed to unsettle all the others.

Skydancer arrived and circled above the house and stables to let Moonflight land first. The battered dragon limped in, barely clearing the roof on the western stable block, and practically dropped from the sky. Flapping her wings ineffectually, she staggered and fell onto her belly. Her impetus carried her into the middle of the yard, slewing her around in an uncontrolled slide until she fetched up against the solid stone wall of the well with a grunt, facing the way she had come. She lay with her eyes half closed, her rib cage rising and falling rhythmically as she fought for breath.

Wony and several other hands started forward. "Stand back," Huw snapped. "Give Alberich room to work."

The dragonleech nodded. He strode rapidly across the yard and began running his hands over Moonflight's flanks. "You! Boy!" He jerked his head at the nearest hand, who happened to be Drane. With a quick despairing glance at Wony, Drane ran across the cobbles. Alberich rapped out terse instructions, and Drane carefully held Moonflight's lacerated wing away from her body so that the dragonleech could feel underneath. Wony watched in horrified fascination as drops of purple dragon blood dripped from the injured wing onto Drane's hand. He flinched but didn't let go.

With a clap of wings, Skydancer alighted on the other side of the stable yard. Breena slipped from his back and hobbled across to Moonflight as fast as her own injuries would allow. She threw herself to the ground beside her dragon and cradled Moonflight's great head in her arms. Her eyes streamed with tears. "Moony," she sobbed. "Oh, Moony, I'm sorry . . . I'm so sorry. . . ."

Cara climbed down from the saddle. Skydancer was making worried crooning noises at the back of his throat. Cara stroked his eye ridges to calm him, with hands that trembled despite all her efforts to control them.

No one moved. No one spoke. All eyes were on Alberich as he examined Moonflight, testing bone and muscle for damage. Occasionally he would call upon Drane to move a wing or raise a leg. Ignoring the blood, which was now liberally staining his tunic, Drane did as he was bid calmly and with an unexpected gentleness. He even held Moonflight's mouth open for the dragonleech's inspection.

At length, Alberich slipped his fingers beneath the dragon's left foreleg and held them there for some time.

Then he straightened up. Breena stared at him as she might at an executioner, waiting for the blow to fall.

"Her heart's racing," Alberich said dispassionately. "Over seventy beats a minute. She's exhausted and in shock. A good deal of muscle strain. Apart from that, as far as I can tell . . ." Breena closed her eyes. ". . . no internal damage, no bones broken, no serious loss of blood. The tears in her sails are painful but superficial. Given the correct care, I see no reason why she shouldn't make a rapid recovery."

Breena let out her breath in a great, juddering sigh, and buried her face against Moonflight's cheek.

"Come along, lad." Alberich gave Drane an appraising look. "Let's get this beast back to her stable." He took the head harness, and Moonflight struggled painfully to her feet. Breena began to follow.

"Breena." Huw's voice was sharp. "Alberich can care for Moonflight for a few moments." A stern glance from the Dragonmaster reminded the spectators that there was work to be done, and they dispersed, conversing in low voices.

Huw waited until they had gone before speaking. "Well? What happened?"

"It was my fault, Dragonmaster." Now that she knew Moonflight's injuries were not as serious as she had feared, Breena's courage had returned.

"It was my fault," she said again. "I wanted to go hunting. Cara tried to stop me. I wouldn't listen." Breena told Huw exactly what had happened in a flat, calm voice, sparing herself nothing.

There was silence when Breena had finished.

"Hunting!" snarled Galen, putting a world of scorn into the exclamation.

Gerda bustled forward. "Leave the poor girl alone, Galen. Can't you see she's at the end of her tether?"

"So she should be!" Galen was furious. "Calls herself a dragonrider. Pesters me for a place in the guard flight. Ha! She's not fit to fly in the nursery hollow. If she hadn't been very, very lucky today . . ."

Breena hung her head and Galen made a visible effort to control his anger.

"Hunters fly in threes," he rasped. "There's a reason for that. If one is injured, another stays, and the third goes for help. Suppose Moonflight hadn't been able to fly? You'd have left Cara with an impossible choice—stay and protect you, or go, knowing that by the time she got back, firedogs, howlers—even pards—might have left nothing for her to find but bones. No rider worth a spit in the fire ever puts another rider in that position."

"All right; you've said your piece and that's enough." Gerda planted her ample form between Galen and Breena. In her own way, Dragonsdale's housekeeper was as formidable as the leader of its guard flight. Galen glared at her, but said no more. Gerda turned to Breena. "Go and see to your dragon, lovie," she said in softer tones.

"Then come into the kitchen. Good hot soup's the best thing for shock, with a nice hot bath after." She patted Breena's shoulder, then headed back to the kitchen.

Breena stood motionless for a moment, biting her lip. Then, without a word, she turned and headed toward Moonflight's stable.

"Half-witted girl," muttered Galen. He turned to Huw. "I hope you'll give that young fool good reason to rue this day's work, Dragonmaster."

Huw gazed after Breena, the severity of his expression tempered with understanding. "Nothing I can do would punish her more severely than she is already punishing herself."

As soon as she had untacked Skydancer and given him a perfunctory grooming, Cara hurried to Moonflight's stall. By the light of a lantern, Breena and Drane were wiping the blood from Moonflight's tattered wings and body, working with great care and gentleness. Cara leaned on the bottom door and watched, fascinated, as Drane dropped his bloodstained cloth in a pail of water, scooped a handful of thorn-apple salve from a pot, and began to spread it over the damaged sail. Moonflight flinched as the astringent mixture cleansed the wound, then sighed with relief as its numbing effect soothed away the pain of torn flesh and muscles.

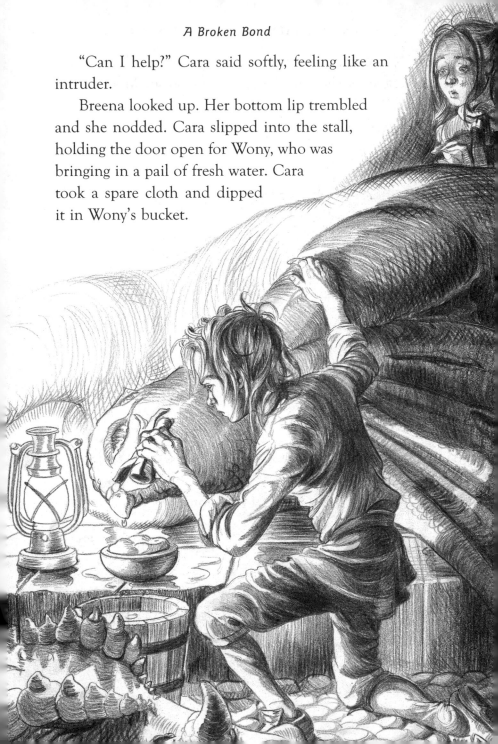

"Can I help?" Cara said softly, feeling like an intruder.

Breena looked up. Her bottom lip trembled and she nodded. Cara slipped into the stall, holding the door open for Wony, who was bringing in a pail of fresh water. Cara took a spare cloth and dipped it in Wony's bucket.

"I thought you were scared of dragons," she said to Drane as she wiped dried blood from Moonflight's flank.

Drane didn't pause in his work. "It's different when they're hurt," he said. "I used to do this on the farm, back home, before I came here—look after sick animals, I mean. Kine, sheep—I was quite good at it, I think. A dragon is just a big animal, after all."

Watching the tenderness with which Drane's usually clumsy hands moved over the injured dragon's hide, Cara had to admit that he seemed to know what he was doing.

A muffled sob from Breena broke her train of thought. She threw her arms around her friend. "Breena, don't cry. It's going to be all right—you heard Alberich. Moony's going to be fine. See, she's feeling better already. Cheer up—it'll all look better in the morning."

But it didn't look better in the morning, or for many mornings after that.

Alberich had been right: Moonflight's injuries had cleared up quickly. Dragons were tough creatures, their bodies designed to repair damage with the minimum delay.

"Moony's looking well," Cara had said to Mistress Hildebrand on the morning Breena led her dragon out into the yard for the first time since the accident. "Apart from a few scars on her sails, you'd never know she'd been hurt."

"Maybe so," Mistress Hildebrand had replied. "But some injuries take longer to heal."

Cara had been annoyed at what sounded like a typical Hildebrand prophecy of doom, and ignored it. But as time went on, and the prophecy seemed to be proving true, she became increasingly concerned. Breena and Moonflight were flying together again a few weeks after their accident, but they were not flying well. With the showing at Drakelodge rapidly approaching, their performances in the practice ring were little short of woeful. Moonflight had developed a habit of refusing obstacles, or flying them so badly that the rigging crew was beginning to complain of overwork.

"What's gone wrong?" Cara asked Mistress Hildebrand as they watched Breena pull Moonflight up and away from a set of horizontal rods after yet another refusal. "Breena's never flown so badly in her life, and Moonflight's as jumpy as a peryton."

"Confidence," said Mistress Hildebrand sharply. "Or rather, lack of it. There are five main reasons for a dragon to refuse an obstacle." She ticked them off on her fingers. "Bad riding, pain, disobedience, tiredness . . . and fear. That wretched accident of theirs has damaged the Trustbond between them. It's not something that's easily repaired."

Cara nodded. "Moonflight wanted to break off the hunt, but Breena set her at a gap that was too small. . . ."

"Exactly. Now Moonflight is refusing obstacles, or flying them poorly, because she's lost confidence in Breena's judgment, and Breena isn't taking them with any conviction because she's lost confidence in her own."

"But they will get their Trustbond back, won't they?" asked Cara anxiously.

"Yes, and it will strengthen with every passing day." Mistress Hildebrand's brow was furrowed. "But will it ever be as strong as before? That I don't know. And the harder she pushes to regain her dragon's trust, the longer it will take. Cara, try and persuade her to relax and take things slowly. It's the only way."

Cara had taken these words to heart, but gradually she had become aware that whenever she tried to persuade Breena and Moonflight to join her and Sky on a practice flight, or just for a grooming session, they always seemed to be busy doing something else. And whenever Cara did manage to get Breena on her own and try to pass on Mistress Hildebrand's advice, Breena would look at her so oddly that she would stumble over the words, lose her thread, and eventually give up.

"Poor Breena," she whispered into Skydancer's ear as she groomed him after another practice session in which Moonflight had knocked down more obstacles than she'd cleared. "I don't know what to do, Sky—I want to help her, but she won't let me."

Sky gave a sympathetic warble.

"She still hasn't qualified for the Island Championships," Cara went on, "and there are only three showings left." She stroked Sky's eye ridge. "I'm afraid for her, Sky. It matters so much to her—and she's running out of time."

HORTENSE MAKES MISCHIEF

On the day of the Drakelodge showing, after another perfect round in the Intermediate Clear, Cara landed Sky in the paddock to find Breena and Moonflight looking so down in the mouth that all pleasure in her own achievement instantly evaporated. Absently, she accepted the congratulations of the other competitors (even Ernestina, who had also flown clear, gave her a chilly nod) before hurrying over to Breena with her face set in an encouraging grin.

"Three clears so far," she told Breena cheerily. "Me, Ernestina, and Ferris from Drakelodge. Your turn next and then I'll see you in the fly-off!"

"I don't think so." Breena's voice was low and her eyes downcast. "Not today."

Cara's heart sank, but she kept her voice light. "Oh, come on! You know you and Moony can do it. Try doing what you always tell me to do—just go out there and enjoy it."

Breena didn't look up. "Cara, I . . ." She took a deep breath. "Look, I'll be fine. Just leave me alone—all right?"

Cara was shocked. "Oh, yes . . . all right," she stuttered. "Well—good luck."

Breena made no reply. Feeling hurt, Cara led Sky back to his place in the picket lines. She failed to notice that Hortense had witnessed Breena's harsh response to her attempt at sympathy and was grinning like a weasel in a moorcock's nest.

Cara made sure Sky was settled, then hurried to the show ring so she could watch Breena's round. Leaning over the wooden fence, she glanced around at the sizable crowd before noticing a familiar figure standing at the edge of the arena half a dragonlength away.

"Drane! What are you doing down here?"

Drane wandered over with a big grin on his face. "I'm a ring-rat!" he said happily.

"I thought you were supposed to be a squirrelman again, up on the top crosspiece."

"So did I, but when I reported to Drakelodge's chief rigger, he said there was no way he'd ever let a scrawny, knock-kneed, straw-brained incompetent like me up one of his masts."

"How rude! I hope you told him off."

"Are you kidding? I shook his hand. I'd have offered to marry his daughter if he had one!" Drane was almost dancing with relief. "Being a ring-rat suits me just fine.

Picking up poles is a lot less dangerous than dangling from a mast, and you're less likely to end up as flat as one of Gerda's drop scones."

Cara smiled. "Let's hope you'll have a nice rest during Breena's round."

"How is she?" asked Drane.

"Feeling the pressure. There's already three of us through to the fly-off. She needs to fly clear to join us." Cara broke off as a round of applause broke out, signaling Breena and Moony's entrance into the arena.

"Got to go," said Drane. "Fingers crossed." As he headed toward the center of the arena to join the other ring-rats, an expectant hush fell over the crowd. The bell rang to begin the round, and Breena set her dragon at the first obstacle.

Cara's hands gripped the fence tightly. "Come on, Breena," she whispered. "You can do this, I know you can."

As Breena successfully guided Moonflight through the opening set of vertical parallel poles, Cara gave a shout of encouragement and urged her friend to continue her good start.

The next obstacle was a straightforward horizontal double, which Sky and Cara had cleared easily. But Breena's approach was labored and unsure. Her hands and legs twitched at Moonflight's reins, sending conflicting signals to the dragon. Moonflight reacted to Breena's indecision by veering too far to the right. She careered into the wooden rods, sending them

tumbling to the
ground.

Cara's stomach
turned. That was it for
Breena—her attempt
to reach the fly-off and
qualify for the Island
Championships was
finished before it had really
begun. Cara shook her
head. She could imagine how
disappointed Breena must be
feeling, knowing that it was
pointless to continue but having
to do so all the same. She could
hardly bear to watch the rest of
the round.

Breena and Moonflight were
flying like beginners, rider and
dragon struggling to find any
rhythm. Moonflight clipped
another obstacle and sent
it plummeting earthward,
directly toward Drane.
With an almighty thump,
it embedded itself upright in
the turf, inches away from his nose.
Drane stared white-faced at the swaying

rod that had come within an ace of skewering him like a roast quail.

Breena's miserable round continued as she pushed Moonflight toward a narrow vertical parallel. In her desperation to finish the round and get away from the critical gaze of the spectators, Breena kicked Moonflight on, urging her to increase speed. Cara's heart sank. *It's only a small gap*, she thought. *Breena's going too fast from too far out.*

Her fears were warranted. In the beating of a wing, Moonflight was upon the obstacle, but far too quickly. At the very last second the dragon spooked, pulled out of her approach, and shot to the left of the poles.

Cara bit her lip. A refusal—five more penalties! "Poor Breena," she murmured, before adding, "and poor Moony."

Breena regained control of Moonflight, flew her back around the pylon, and headed for the parallel a second time. Again, the dragon didn't like the look of the small gap between the poles and refused once more, this time banking off to the right. The crowd below let out a huge groan.

Cara was feeling wretched. One more refusal and Breena would be disqualified—something that had never happened to her before—and what would Galen say about that? She couldn't bear to think about it.

The same thoughts were clearly passing through Breena's head, and her struggles with Moonflight became more frantic. But it was all to no avail. Moonflight wanted nothing to do with the obstacle and fought desperately against her rider.

Watching helplessly, Cara was in torment. "Come on, Moony, come on," she pleaded. Then she gave a gasp of horror, hardly able to believe what she was seeing: Breena had taken a hand off the reins and reached down into the saddle pocket to produce a riding whip.

"Oh, no," whispered Cara. "No, Breena, don't . . ."

With only one hand on the reins, Breena was being thrown from side to side. Only her safety belt was keeping her in her saddle. She tightened her hold of the small black leather crop and raised it.

Cara felt physically sick. Surely Breena wasn't going to hit Moonflight? If she did, she would be breaking a cardinal rule of Dragonsdale: Never hit a dragon in anger. Her days at the stables would be numbered.

Breena raised the whip high above Moonflight's flank. For a moment she held it poised, hesitating.

Then she lowered it and pulled the dragon out of the approach, bringing her flight to a voluntary conclusion.

Cara almost fainted with relief.

To a smattering of consolatory applause, Breena guided Moony from the ring, her face set solid as granite.

Anxious to commiserate with her friend, Cara dashed to the exit gate, where she found Breena still sitting on her disconsolate dragon, tears streaming down her face.

"Breena . . ." Cara stopped as words failed her. What could she say? Perhaps she should try and let Breena know that the refusal wasn't her fault. "That double . . . Moony must have been thinking about the gap between the pine trees when you were hunting the—"

"I know what she was thinking about," snapped Breena, wiping at her tears. "I don't need to be told."

Cara put her hand up to Breena's stirrup. "She will learn to trust you again—she will. I know it's hard, but you have to give her time—"

"Oh, I daresay. How much time would you like with one less rival to worry about?" Breena jabbed her heels into Moonflight's flanks and urged her toward the paddock.

Cara stood and watched her go, too shocked to speak.

"Cara! Cara! Sixth place!" Wony was running across the paddock toward her. "My first time in a Clear Flight and I only had three obstacles down! Bumble was brilliant!"

"Oh—well done," said Cara distractedly.

Wony's face fell at Cara's lack of enthusiasm. "Well, it was a pretty good result for my first time out," she said. "I thought you'd be pleased."

"Oh, Wony," replied Cara. "I'm sorry, it's just that—"

"Didn't you fly clear?" Wony cut in. "Has someone else won?"

Cara shook her head. "No, I flew clear. It's Breena." She began to tell Wony about their friend's disastrous performance.

In the ring, Drane was sweating after the exertion of first dodging the fallout from Breena's round, then carrying the wooden poles and putting them back in their slings.

The announcer raised his megaphone. "And riding for Clapperclaw on Silvercloud, the High Lord's daughter, Hortense." The bell rang to start the next round.

"Oh, no," groaned Drane. "Every silver cloud has a dark lining! Here we go again. . . ." He cast an envious glance at the nearest squirrelman standing high up on his mast, comfortably out of harm's way.

He didn't have to wait long. True to form, Hortense clattered into the first, second, and fourth obstacles, followed by the sixth, seventh, and eighth. It was spectacularly awful riding, even for Hortense.

On the ground, Drane and his fellow ring-rats scurried around, living up to their nickname as the poles rained down around them like spears on a battlefield. "Every time," muttered Drane as he struggled with a rod that had embedded itself into the turf. "Every blessed time . . ." He gave a cry of alarm as yet another pole came crashing to the ground just feet away from him. "And I thought squirrelmen were nuts," he moaned. "I didn't know how good I had it!"

Finally, Hortense completed her round and exited the ring, leaving behind a scene of devastation. In the stand, Lord Torin was huffing and puffing for all he was worth. "Can't understand it! Whuff! What's going on? Whuff! Must be the course design. The girl's not that bad, what! She always wins the practice sessions at Clapperclaw. Top notch, every time, whuff!"

Mistress Hildebrand, sitting directly behind the High Lord, privately thought that Hortense could only have won the practice sessions if the other Clapperclaw riders had been under orders from Dragonmaster Adair to let her win, but decided that it would not be tactful to share this view.

"Whuff! Terrible course, terrible," moaned Torin. "I'll have a word with the judges! Make 'em see sense, what!" Mistress Hildebrand rolled her eyes as Torin continued to moan about the course's shortcomings to all who were willing to listen (and to those who didn't want to listen but had no choice).

Back at the picket line, Wony was helping Cara check over Skydancer's tack, ready for the fly-off against Ernestina and Ferris. The winner of the gold rosette would be the rider with the fewest penalties—or, if there was a tie, whoever had completed the course in the fastest time. The fly-off would be fiercely competitive, and the last thing Cara could afford was a broken strap or belt.

Wony finished checking Sky's stirrup irons and turned her head toward the paddock. "Do you think I should go and talk to Breena?"

Cara shook her head. "No, it's best that she's on her own. Let her have time to calm down."

"All right." The younger girl gave Cara a hug. "Fly well."

Cara smiled and put on her riding helmet and goggles before climbing up Sky's foreleg and settling into the saddle. A bell rang, and the announcer called for the three riders in the fly-off to make their way to the ring.

In the paddock, Breena was wiping Moonflight down with a cloth after their exertions in the arena. She paused briefly to listen to the voice of the event announcer.

"First to go—he's a local boy, so let's give him a big hand—Ferris of Drakelodge!" The crowd applauded enthusiastically.

"Not watching the fly-off?"

Breena turned to see Hortense. She went back to her task, saying nothing.

Hortense ignored the rebuff and continued, her voice sickly sweet. "I thought you'd be supporting Cara—you know, the honor of Dragonsdale and all that."

Breena remained quiet and continued wiping at Moonflight's flank. A groan of disappointment from the arena signaled that Ferris of Drakelodge had brought down an obstacle.

"Well, it's only a silly competition, isn't it?" prattled Hortense. "I mean, it isn't a matter of life and death."

"What do you want, Hortense?"

"Want? What makes you think I want anything?" Hortense looked the very picture of wounded innocence. "I only stopped by to say that I was sorry to see you riding like that—it wasn't like you and Moonflight at all. Hitting all those obstacles and refusing fences! 'That's not like Breena at all,' I said to all my friends."

Breena's eyes closed against the tears of humiliation that threatened to destroy her outward calm. She could just see Hortense doing this, and enjoying every minute of it.

"Then I heard about your little . . ." Hortense paused momentarily, as if trying to find the correct word. ". . . accident! And then it all became clear!" She sighed deeply and shook her head. "Dragonmaster Adair says that after a flying accident, it takes ages for a rider and dragon to regain their Trustbond."

"Does he?" said Breena through gritted teeth.

"Oh, yes, it's a well-known fact," replied Hortense earnestly. She broke off to listen to the next announcement.

"That was Ferris of Drakelodge riding Suncatcher, with ten penalties in a time of three and a half minutes. Next to go is Stormbringer, ridden by Ernestina of Clapperclaw."

The crowd applauded generously.

"Ernestina is a good rider," said Hortense. "She used to beat you quite often, didn't she?"

Breena's lips tightened, but she still refused to give Hortense the satisfaction of provoking her into a bitter response.

Hortense shook her head. "But even she isn't up to Cara's standard. It's so much more difficult for anyone else to win gold now that Cara and Skydancer are around." She gave a little throwaway laugh. "You must yearn for the old days before Cara was allowed to fly. . . ." She left the suggestion hanging in the air.

A loud groan from the crowd signaled a failure by Ernestina.

"Ten penalties," said Hortense. "It looks as though all Cara has to do is fly clear and it's another gold!" She let out a deep sigh. "Cara and Skydancer—what a team—formidable, you might say! Just like her mother . . . Champion of Champions, three times. No one else even had a chance!" Hortense paused, her eyes narrowing, trying to determine what effect her words were having.

Hortense's implication was not lost on Breena: If Cara continued to overshadow her, what hope would she have of ever winning the Island Championships and joining the guard flight?

A bell rang to end the round. The announcer's voice echoed from the arena. "Ten penalties in a time of three and a quarter minutes for Ernestina and Stormbringer. If Cara of Dragonsdale can fly clear, the gold rosette will be hers for a third successive showing."

Hortense, who had been listening with her head to one side, nodded wisely. "What did I tell you?" she said brightly. "Just like her mother! Maybe we should go down to the arena and see Cara win . . . ?"

Breena remained still. The High Lord's daughter gave her a couple of moments to listen to the applause ringing out for Cara and Skydancer's entrance.

"Breena—?" She broke off. "Oh, it doesn't matter. . . ."

"What doesn't matter?" snapped Breena.

"Nothing . . . I was just thinking . . . no, it isn't important."

Breena's hands tightened. "Spit it out, Hortense."

"Oh, if you insist. I was just worried about you not qualifying for the Island Championships, but then I realized that there are still the showings at Clapperclaw and Dragonsdale to come, so there's time for you to sort it all out between you and Moonflight."

"Yes, there is," said Breena flatly.

"And then there's next year as well."

"What do you mean?"

"Well, if this season's showings are a write-off, you can always qualify next year. . . ."

Breena's whole body tensed.

"Oh, silly me!" Hortense's air of mock embarrassment was worthy of a prize. "I forgot—this is the last year that you can enter as a junior rider, isn't it?" She paused, allowing Breena to contemplate her situation before delivering the final blow. "And it would be such a shame if you didn't qualify for the championships, because then Galen won't have you in the guard flight, will he?"

Breena bit her lip to stifle a sob.

Seeing that her words had achieved the desired effect, Hortense gave an airy laugh. "Ah well, as I said, I'm sure you'll sort everything out. I daresay I'll be seeing you—here and there."

As Hortense began to walk away, a sustained round of applause and cheering broke out, all but drowning the announcer's voice. "A clear round! A clear round and the gold rosette for Cara of Dragonsdale and Skydancer!"

Hortense turned back to face Breena. "She's good, isn't she? A real competitor—always having to win, and not letting anyone or anything stand in her way. Not even friends . . ." And with that, Hortense gave a little wave and skipped off, leaving Breena quivering with anger and dismay.

BEST OF
ENEMIES

"Come on, Breena! Race you back to Dragonsdale!"

After the flying at Drakelodge was over, Cara had been looking forward to the rest of the day. Every stable tried to make its own showing the best on the island, and all the stables vied with one another to see which could produce the most lavish food and the most spectacular entertainment. This was one area where, Cara was forced to admit, Dragonsdale lagged behind some of its rivals. At a Dragonsdale showing, Gerda's food was always so sumptuous as to make the tables groan—almost as loudly as the diners who had been tempted to eat far too much of it—but the entertainment was usually fairly low-key, as Huw took no interest in such things. But Dragonmaster Lunn did, and the Drakelodge showing always attracted the best bards and minstrels in Seahaven.

Cara could hardly wait for the celebrations to start. But when she'd gone to find Breena, Moonflight was already saddled and ready to go, and Breena hadn't wanted to stay.

"All right," Cara had said. "I'll fly back with you."

"There's no need," Breena had replied. "You stay and enjoy the dancing and everything. I'll be fine."

But Cara had insisted, and Breena had given in, rather ungraciously. On the flight back, Cara had called out cheery remarks about the events of the day, but Breena had just slumped in the saddle, replying (when she replied at all) with brief, disinterested nods, until Cara had gotten fed up and proposed a race.

For a moment, she thought Breena would refuse, but then she gave Cara a savage grin, flicked the reins, and dug her heels into Moonflight's flanks. The startled dragon leapt ahead.

Cara crouched in the saddle. "Come on, Sky! Let's show them!"

At Cara's urging, Sky went into a dive, gaining speed and sculling through the air with his great wings while the wind rushing past Cara's ears rose in pitch from a hiss to a howl. The wastes of Clonmoor flashed below them, their dull browns now mixed with vivid purple from the early flowering of the heather. By the time they reached the Tumblewater, the dragons were neck and neck as they raced through the spray thrown up by its thundering waters. But over the gentler fields of the farmland surrounding Dragonsdale, Skydancer stretched away, and Cara flew triumphantly into the stable yard a good forty dragonlengths ahead of her friend. As Breena brought Moonflight in to land, Cara tore off her helmet and goggles, laughing. "Beat you!"

Breena alighted from Moonflight's back, slowly removed her helmet, and lowered her goggles so that they hung around her neck. She turned to Cara with a strange expression on her face—a smile that was so

sad and twisted that it was no smile at all.

"Cara," she said, "do you have to win all the time?"

Then she turned away and led Moonflight back to her stable without another word.

"What's wrong with them?" Drane leaned on his broom and looked first at Breena, then at Cara. He had to turn his head to do this as the two girls were grooming their dragons in opposite corners of the yard, ostentatiously keeping as much distance between themselves as they possibly could without leaving the stables altogether.

Wony set down her wheelbarrow—carefully, because even fresh dragon droppings could explode if handled roughly—and brushed the hair out of her eyes. "I don't know. They're barely speaking to each other. They've been like this ever since they got back from Drakelodge."

"But why?" asked Drane. "They always used to do everything together. Nowadays they don't even sit next to each other for lunch."

Wony shook her head; the jealousies that were souring the relationship between the older girls were beyond her understanding.

So Drane decided to tackle Cara. The next afternoon, as they were taking an inventory of the feed store, he asked her bluntly what was wrong between her and Breena.

"Nothing," Cara said in offhand tones. "That's seventy-three brace of moorcocks and eighty-four of boobries. . . ."

"Oh, come on! You've fallen out over something."

"I haven't fallen out with anybody. And twenty haunches of peryton—twenty-one, twenty-two, twenty-three . . ."

"Then why isn't Breena talking to you?"

"Oh—now you've made me lose count!"

"Don't change the subject. Why?"

"You'd better ask her. Now, we have fifty-seven bags of feed—oh, no, fifty-eight, there's one hidden under that pile of empty sacks. . . ."

"Well, then, why aren't you talking to her?"

"I am talking to her. I talk to her whenever she talks to me."

"But she doesn't talk to you!"

"I can't help that. How many bags of feed did I say?"

"I don't know."

"Well, how many have you written down?"

"Oh—was I supposed to be writing all that down?"

After that, Drane tried to tackle Breena. The responses he got were just the same as those he'd gotten from Cara, only more so. The upshot of all this was that by the time Drane had given up making his "tactful" inquiries, Cara and Breena were not only not talking to each other, they were barely talking to him, either.

A couple of days later, Drane stayed behind when the kitchen emptied after lunch and actually volunteered to help with the washing-up. This unexpected development so flummoxed Gerda that she had to sit down for a moment and flap herself with her apron.

"Gerda," Drane said as he scrubbed at a pan that looked as if it had been used for boiling glue, "do you know what's wrong with Breena and Cara?"

Gerda gave him a shrewd glance. "Least said, soonest mended. You missed a spot."

Drane sighed and gave up all pretense of scrubbing. "Oh, don't you go all mysterious on me as well. I'm worried about them, and I don't know who else to ask. I've tried talking to them . . ."

"And found you may as well have saved your breath to cool your porridge." Gerda tapped Drane on the chest with a ladle. "You won't make anything better by interfering. Just leave them alone and they'll sort it out sooner or later."

"I suppose it's girl stuff and I wouldn't understand."

"No, it's dragonrider stuff, and anyone with half a brain—" Gerda broke off and sighed. "Oh, I suppose we'd better get this sorted out, otherwise you'll just keep on asking questions and making it worse. Listen, lad," she continued in kindlier tones, "last year, Breena was our best junior rider. Everyone looked to her to win for Dragonsdale. Even if she didn't win, she was up against riders she knew she could beat if everything went right. But then Cara started to ride and everything changed."

"You mean, Breena's jealous of Cara?"

Gerda rolled her eyes. "Yes, but it's more complicated than that. If you go thinking that Breena is just being sulky and a poor loser, you'll have the wrong idea altogether. Breena doesn't mind losing—well, not beyond reason—as long as she knows she can win. But when she flies against Cara, she knows that she can't win. That's the point."

"But Cara's her friend."

"That only makes matters worse. Breena's been trying all season not to be jealous of Cara—I've seen her struggling with her feelings many a time—and she knows it's wrong and mean of her, but she can't help it. So, even now that they've fallen out, she hates herself much more than she thinks she hates Cara. And if what I hear is true—and it usually is—that nasty little madam Hortense has been stirring things up between them as well."

"And Breena's flying so badly at the moment. I don't suppose that helps." Drane thought for a moment. "Is winning that important to her?"

"Yes, because that fool Galen—" Gerda broke off and stamped her foot in exasperation. "There! Now you've made me speak ill of your betters. But he is a fool for all that, telling Breena he won't let her into the guard flight unless she wins the Island Championships. She knows she can't do that, and she's desperate to be in the guard flight, and it's Cara who stands between her and the thing she wants most in her whole life—and you wonder why the two of them aren't getting along? Use your eyes more and your mouth less, young man, is my advice."

At that moment the door crashed open and Mistress Hildebrand's booming voice echoed around the kitchen, rattling the pots on their shelves and the pans on their hooks. "This time, I am definitely going to resign! Gerda, is there any bramble tea left in the pot?"

Drane took one look at Mistress Hildebrand's angry countenance and busied himself at the sink. Suds flew left and right. Gerda rolled her eyes and heaved herself to her feet. "It'll be stewed. Sit down—it won't take me a minute to make a fresh pot."

"Thank you." Hildebrand slapped her riding whip down on the table with a snap that made Drane jump. "I don't know what is wrong with those two!"

Her apron wrapped around her hands, Gerda carefully lifted the heavy kettle from the hob. "Which two?"

"Cara and Breena!"

The kettle slipped from Gerda's grasp and clattered back onto the hob. She and Drane exchanged startled glances.

"What about them?" asked Gerda.

Hildebrand gave an exasperated sigh. "My two singleton riders, Caley and Tomey, have had to drop out of the display team. They let their dragons clip wings in training this morning, careless young oafs! The poor beasts won't be fit to fly at the Clapperclaw showing, and probably not at Dragonsdale, either." Gerda poured boiling water into the teapot while Hildebrand continued. "So I've just told Cara and Breena that they'll be flying in the formation team instead. I thought they'd be pleased! But they looked as if I'd given them a week's extra mucking-out duties."

She reached for the mug of tea proffered by a poker-faced Gerda. "I swear—ooh, that's hot!—I swear I don't know what's going through their heads sometimes."

Several days later, Drane and Wony were dangling their feet in the Dragonsbeck, watching Hortense tether her dragon to the hitching rail outside Wayland's Forge, when Cara came drifting along the bank from the house.

"Hello," she said listlessly. "What are you looking at?"

"Hortense. She's here again." Drane kicked at the water, sending a splash of silvery droplets across the stream. "She seems to be around a lot these days."

Cara watched as Hortense disappeared into the forge. "I don't remember seeing her as often as this when she was riding for us. If she likes the place so much, why did she leave?"

Drane shrugged. "She's always got one reason or another—she's ordering something from Wayland or Merril Leatherworker."

Cara sat down beside Wony and took off her boots, throwing them onto the grass. "It sounds as if she's making excuses—she could send a servant on that sort of errand. I wonder what she's up to."

"I've seen her hanging around the stables watching Breena . . . and I've seen her watching you as well." Drane gave Cara a sideways glance.

"Me?" Cara shook her head. "I can't imagine what Hortense could possibly want with me."

Eyeing Cara carefully, Drane said, "Do you think we should warn Breena?"

"About what?" Cara snorted. "Maybe Breena likes having Hortense around. If they want to be friends, it's got nothing to do with me."

Wony burst into tears.

Cara was shocked. "Wony!" She put her arms around the smaller girl's shoulders. "What is it? What's wrong?"

"You are! You and Breena." When her sobs had died down enough for her to make sense, Wony went on, "Everything was so lovely before, and now it's all horrible because you and Breena have fallen out, and I don't know why."

"Well, don't ask me," said Cara crossly. "She was foul to me when we got back from Drakelodge, even though I left early just to fly home with her, and she's been foul ever since. I don't know what's the matter with her."

"I do," said a cool voice from the bank behind them. Hortense had left the forge and slipped up behind them unobserved.

Cara looked up with a scowl. "Nobody asked you," she said sharply. "What are you doing here, anyway?"

"Ordering some buckles from your Forgemaster, if it's any business of yours. Anyway," Hortense continued with a superior smirk, "it's obvious what's the matter with Breena. She's jealous. She hates it when you win all the time."

"Don't judge everyone by your own standards," said Drane.

Hortense's eyes flashed, but she kept her voice level. "There's no need to be rude. I'm only mentioning this as a friend."

"As a . . . ?" Hortense's effrontery left Cara speechless.

"It's so unfair," Hortense continued blithely. "You can't help it if you and Skydancer are so much better than her and Moonflight."

Drane stood up. "This has nothing to do with you. Why don't you go away and stop poking your long nose in where it isn't wanted?"

"Don't talk to me like that, stable boy," snarled Hortense. With an effort, she regained control of herself. "I'm going. Just don't say I didn't warn you," she told Cara. "It isn't nice when you find out that the person you thought was your best friend is plotting against you."

Cara stared after Hortense's retreating figure. "What did she mean by that?"

"Oh, for pity's sake!" snapped Drane. "You're not taking any notice of anything Hortense says, are you?"

Cara hurriedly shook her head. "No—no, of course not."

But Hortense's words came back to haunt Cara over the days that followed. She remembered them every time Breena ignored her, or sat somewhere else at mealtimes, or went off with Moonflight on her own.

"Breena is being such a pain," she told Sky as she rubbed the dust from his scales after a particularly unsuccessful session of formation flying. Cara didn't want to believe that Breena wasn't her friend anymore, but time passed, and as the nagging doubts persisted, it became easier for Cara to forget the events that had made Breena so unhappy, and harder to feel sympathy for her.

"I mean," she went on, "she looks at me as if I'm something the wyvern dragged in. She hardly ever talks to me, and when she does, all she wants to do is complain about something to do with the display team. She moans like a dragon with colic if I make a mistake, but she makes mistakes all the time, and if I quietly draw her attention to them, she bites my head off." Sky gave an unhappy hoot and Cara scratched his eye ridge. "Oh, I'm sorry, Sky. I know it's not your fault. It's just—there's no one else I can talk to. Drane's being sniffy with me, and when I asked him why, he said he was fed up to the back teeth with Breena and me snapping at each other and he didn't see any reason why he should be involved in our squabbles. I told him Breena was doing the squabbling, not me, and he just walked off. Even Wony's avoiding me these days."

Cara's eyes stung. "I hate feeling this way about Breena, but she's being so horrible to me and I haven't done anything wrong! If she wants to be stupid and jealous because we're flying well and she and Moony aren't, there's nothing I can do about it." She flung her arms around Sky's neck and hugged him. "You're the only one I can talk to, Sky." Tears splashed onto the dragon's scales, shining where they fell.

As time went on, the arguments, angry looks, and cold, bitter silences continued, and like Breena, Cara began spending as much of her free time as possible away from Dragonsdale. So it was that, one bright summer's day in Shearingtide, she flew Skydancer to a lonely beach on Merfolk Bay.

They came in to land at the water's edge. The sand beneath Skydancer's talons was wet; high water had come and gone, and the tide was going out. Waves broke with a boom and a long, echoing roar like distant thunder, hissing as they met the sand. The sun shone in a cloudless sky of duck-egg blue.

The warmth, the regular, soothing beat of the sea, and the plaintive cries of the seabirds made Cara feel sleepy. She slipped from the saddle, and had just begun to unbuckle the belly strap so that Sky could go for a splash in the waves without ruining the leather, when a cry of dismay from somewhere nearby made her jump. She let go of the buckle, spun around, and stared in all directions. Sky craned his neck to see where the commotion was coming from.

Cara followed the dragon's gaze and looked out to sea. Beyond the breakers, she saw what looked like a boy rearing out of the water, waving frantically. The boy opened his mouth, and the cry came again.

"Come on, Sky." Cara hastily retightened the buckle. "Let's get out there quickly. Someone's drowning!"

THE MERBOY

Cara brought Sky into a hover just above the struggling boy. The downdraft from the dragon's wing beats ruffled the surface of the sea and flattened the waves.

"Don't worry," she called. "We'll have you out of there in no time!"

It was only then that she became aware that the cries the stranger was making were actually words. His voice was high-pitched and his accent outlandish, but as she listened she found herself able to understand him quite clearly.

"Go away, human girl!" he was calling. "Leave it alone!"

Cara was nonplussed. Why was he calling her "human girl"? Surely he must be human as well. . . .

Realization struck. The stranger wasn't drowning at all. He was thrashing about in the water, beating at it with angry fists. For some reason Cara didn't understand, he was furious with her. Despite this, she was entranced. "You're a merboy!"

The boy shook his fist at her. "You can't have it!"

Cara twisted in the saddle, looking around. "What can't I have?"

"My capricorn! You landed right next to it. Do not

pretend! You will carry it off. Go away!"

Cara was intrigued. She had never seen a capricorn, but she had heard of the goat-headed, fish-tailed creatures that the merpeople herded in the same way that humans herded sheep. But capricorns never left the sea. How could she have landed near it? Unless . . .

"Come on, Sky." Cara flicked the reins. Skydancer gave a hoot of relief; like all dragons, he found hovering tiring. He tilted his wings and went into a glide. Cara turned him back toward the shore. The merboy gave a shrill cry of rage and leapt from the water like a porpoise before swimming rapidly in pursuit.

The lost capricorn wasn't hard to find. It was about the size of a dolphin, with curved, knobbled horns and the strange, slotted eyes of a goat. The top part of its body was covered in sleek white fur like a seal's, and the bottom part with shimmering fish scales. Its flippers were sending fountains of spray up from a rock pool near where Cara and Sky had first landed. It must have been lying quiet when they arrived; ironically, if its owner hadn't panicked and called attention to it, Cara and Sky might not have noticed it at all. Now, perhaps having heard its master's voice, it was bleating piteously.

Cara brought Skydancer in to land close to the pool. She clambered over the surrounding rocks and slipped into the water, which was about waist deep, making the comforting noises she always used with dragonets. "*Cush cush . . . cush cush . . .*" she chirruped, reaching out toward the frightened creature. "Come on, I'm not going to hurt you."

But the capricorn was in no mood to listen to reason. It rolled its eyes at Cara—then, without warning, it leapt through the water and butted her with its curved horns, so hard that she fell back into the pool with an explosive "Whoof!"

"Leave her alone, you—you shark! You're hurting her!" The merboy thrashed about in the sea just beyond the line of breakers.

"I am not—she's hurting me!" Blinking water out of her eyes and muttering darkly to herself, Cara climbed to her feet and stalked the capricorn through the shallow water. The terrified beast tried to butt her again—but Cara had spent a good deal of her life dealing with unruly dragonets and knew tricks worth two of that one. Sidestepping neatly, she caught the capricorn around its middle. "Got you!" she cried.

The merboy gave a bubbling howl of despair.

However, two things quickly became clear. One was that the capricorn wasn't about to calm down. It bleated and wriggled and squirmed so much that it was all Cara could do to hold on to it. The second difficulty was that it was far too heavy for her to carry out of the pool, over the rocks, and across the ever-widening area of beach to the sea without dropping it and hurting it—and if she did drop it, she very much doubted whether she'd be able to pick it up again.

Cara let the capricorn go and it splashed away from her, bleating angrily. She climbed out of the pool and ran to the edge of the waves. Cupping her hands around her mouth, she called, "I'm sorry, it's too heavy. I'll have to go and get help."

The merboy's face twisted with rage. "Yes—bring more human killers! Take my whole flock!"

"I'm not trying to kill your stupid capricorn! I'm trying to help her. Look, it won't take long—I can fetch some kind of a sling and . . ."

But the merboy wasn't listening. He was looking, not at Cara, but at something behind her. "See—your sky-dragon!" He shook his fists again and thrashed his tail in a perfect frenzy.

Cara wheeled around. Skydancer, tired of not being invited to join in the fun, had taken off and was now hovering above the rock pool. As she watched, open-mouthed, the dragon made a grab below the surface and rose into the air with the struggling capricorn clutched in his great talons.

"You will help her—oh, yes! I have seen this sort of 'help' from your kind! Your sky-dragon is helping itself to my capricorns. Thief! Pirate! Bloodsucker!" The merboy was beside himself with rage and despair.

"Don't worry! He won't eat it!" But in fact Cara was by no means sure of this. Dragons weren't supposed to eat farm beasts, and mostly they didn't—at least, as long as they were supervised. But occasionally a dragon left to its own devices would take a sheep or a goat, seemingly deciding that the tasty fresh meat was worth its rider's reproaches. And Cara wasn't certain that Skydancer would even recognize the capricorn as a domestic animal belonging to the merfolk; he might consider it a wild creature, and therefore fair game for a hungry dragon. "I'm sure my—er—sky-dragon means no harm," she said, hoping it was true.

She was intensely relieved when Skydancer flew across the beach to open water, carrying the capricorn, and carefully lowered it to the surface before opening his claws and releasing it. The creature was quite unharmed. It swam rapidly away, bleating with alarm. Several goat heads appeared above the waves. The lost capricorn swam into their midst, to be greeted with a joyful chorus of bleats before the whole group dived and was lost to view.

"Well done, Sky!" Cara waved to Skydancer, who hooted cheerfully and went to perch on a large boulder, watching his rider intently to see what other entertainment she might have devised to keep him amused.

Cara waded out toward the merboy, who had stopped thrashing around and now looked very uncertain. He watched her approach nervously, clearly ready to bolt at the first sign of treachery, but did not retreat.

Cara stopped just close enough to the merboy for normal conversation.

"You spoke truly," he said in wonder. "You did save my capricorn." He seemed at a loss for a moment, then gave a quick nod, never taking his eyes off Cara. "Thank you."

Cara smiled. "It was Sky who did the rescue, not me."

The merboy turned to Skydancer. He thrashed his fish tail so that the human part of his body rose right out of the water, and made a formal bow. "Thank you, friend sky-dragon."

To Cara's astonishment, Sky crouched down and bent his neck, as though returning the bow. She laughed aloud and clapped her hands.

The boy turned back to Cara. "Again, I thank you. If I had lost the capricorn, my father would have been very angry." He began to swim away.

"Wait!" Cara didn't want him to go. She was curious about the merpeople. What's more, this was the first time in days she'd spoken to anybody who wasn't giving her the cold shoulder because of her quarrel with Breena.

The merboy stopped dead in the water and waited with grave courtesy.

Cara asked the first thing that came into her head. "What's your name?"

The boy gave her a guarded smile. "Ronan."

"Mine's Cara. My dragon is called Skydancer." When Ronan made no reply, Cara blurted, "What are you doing here?"

"Why should I not be here?" Ronan spread his arms to take in the sweep of the sea and land all around them. "This is Merfolk Bay."

Cara was flustered. "Oh, yes, of course—it's your home, isn't it? What I meant to ask was, how did your capricorn get caught like that?"

Ronan seemed to relax a little. "I was grazing my flock close inshore," he explained. "Farther out, there are sea lions and leopard seals. They hunt capricorns whenever they can."

Cara looked out to sea, wondering what leopard seals looked like and whether they were as ferocious as the pards that haunted the wild north lands of Seahaven.

"Sometimes," Ronan went on, "the younger capricorns swim too far in to find the tastiest seaweed."

"But if they get caught in a pool, can't you just wait for the tide to come in again so they can swim out?"

Ronan nodded, his face serious. "Sometimes, yes. But sometimes that is too late. If the boat people find our beasts, they kill them."

"You mean the fisherfolk?" Cara sighed. "I know they don't like you."

"And we do not like them! Their nets trap our capricorns and sea cows, and also wild creatures like dolphins and porpoises that do them no harm." Ronan paused, seeming to regret his momentary anger. "But there are other dangers for a stranded beast," he explained in a quieter voice. "Animals come from inland—animals with eyes of fire, four-legged creatures with spikes along their backs . . ."

"Firedogs and howlers." Cara nodded. "They attack our farm animals, too. Even a dragon if it's hurt."

"And sometimes," Ronan said, watching Cara carefully, "our beasts are taken by sky-dragons, like yours."

Cara shook her head. "That can't be right. Dragons don't hunt capricorns—they hunt perytons and wild boar and calygrayhounds. I've never heard of a dragon taking a capricorn."

"But they do," said Ronan fiercely. "I have seen them! And not only stranded ones. They hunt them in the sea, in the heart of our flocks, with bows and lances."

"Not our dragons!" Cara was stung by the accusation. "Not riders from Dragonsdale." Ronan shrugged. Cara fought back her resentment: Of course Ronan could have no idea about the different dragon stables on Seahaven, any more than she could understand the world beneath the sea. "I'm sorry," she said humbly. "I don't want to argue, but I know my father would not allow our dragons to hunt your flocks."

Ronan's bow indicated that he accepted this statement while not necessarily believing it. Cara decided to steer away from the uncomfortable subject. "It must be a strange world you live in," she said. "I mean, a world without birds, or trees, or flowers, or grass."

"It would seem strange to you, no doubt," said Ronan solemnly. "But just as you have sky-dragons, we have sea-dragons. We have fish, which swim through the water as birds fly through the air, and we have birds, too—the ones you call puffins, cormorants, gannets—many kinds. They fly through the water chasing the fish, though they do not stay long. We have forests of kelp, and coral gardens. . . . To us, our world is as rich and varied as, I daresay, yours is to you."

"I'm sure it is," said Cara politely, though she found it hard to believe that the realm of the merfolk could possibly be as beautiful and exciting as the Islands of Bresal. "Please don't think me rude," she went on hesitantly, "but I'm surprised you know our language. Do you speak it among yourselves?"

Ronan smiled. "No, we have our own language."

Cara was intrigued. "What does it sound like?"

"Well . . ." Ronan considered. "Well, for instance, our word for sea is *mor*."

Cara nodded. "Mor," she said, trying out the unfamiliar sound. "Mor."

Ronan indicated the rock on which Skydancer was still perched. "And what you call waves, we call *thonn*."

"Thonn . . ."

"And the land, we call *tir*. So our name for our home is Tir Fo Thonn—The Land Beneath the Waves." The way Ronan pronounced the name in his own tongue, it sounded like the voice of the sea itself, washing against shingle.

"You speak our language very well," said Cara enviously. "I'm afraid I don't speak yours at all."

"We have had dealings with the people you call fisherfolk for many years—though, for a long time now, those dealings have not been friendly. I learned your language at school."

"I didn't know merpeople had schools," said Cara.

Ronan looked surprised. "Of course we do. Porpoises have schools, don't they?"

Cara remembered her lessons on the words for groups of animals: a flight of dragons, a herd of kine, a flock of sheep, a screech of howlers, a school of porpoises. "Er—yes," she said.

"Well? Where do you think they got the idea?" Ronan looked at Cara with a very solemn expression. Then his face split into a broad grin.

Cara's eyes widened. She crowed with delight. "It's a joke!" She laughed until her sides were sore. "You really had me fooled."

Ronan was laughing, too. "Your face! So serious—"

He broke off as Skydancer bugled a warning. Ronan looked up, and his face set into hard lines. "Dragons are coming. They are hunting my flock." He pointed at Cara in accusation. "You are with the raiders!" His voice was bitter. "Liar! Traitor! You pretend to help me, then you keep me talking here so that I cannot protect my beasts!"

Cara was aghast. "No! I swear . . ."

But Ronan had already plunged beneath the waves. Seconds later, a strange creature reared from the sea a little farther out. Its head and body looked something like a dragon's but were colored bright yellow with white stripes. It had huge, shimmering sea-green limbs that were neither legs nor wings nor yet flippers, but something that looked like a mixture of all three, with the waving shapes of seaweed thrown in. It could only be a sea-dragon.

As Cara watched, Ronan leapt from the water to land on the creature's back. The beast gave a strange cry—a sort of bubbling scream like nothing Cara had ever heard before—and dived. Moments later, the merboy and his mount rose from the sea many dragonlengths from where they had

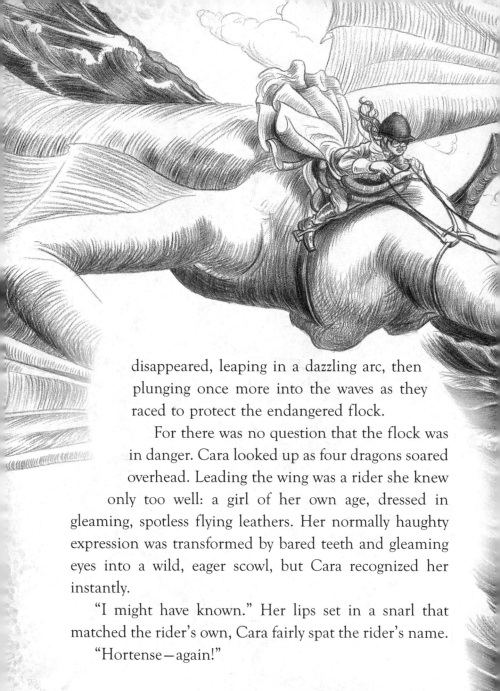

disappeared, leaping in a dazzling arc, then plunging once more into the waves as they raced to protect the endangered flock.

For there was no question that the flock was in danger. Cara looked up as four dragons soared overhead. Leading the wing was a rider she knew only too well: a girl of her own age, dressed in gleaming, spotless flying leathers. Her normally haughty expression was transformed by bared teeth and gleaming eyes into a wild, eager scowl, but Cara recognized her instantly.

"I might have known." Her lips set in a snarl that matched the rider's own, Cara fairly spat the rider's name.

"Hortense—again!"

A FIERY
CHALLENGE

"**S**ky!"

Cara hurried back to the beach, feeling like she was trying to wade through treacle. She shambled, stiff-legged, as fast as she could, desperately thrusting water aside to aid her progress, scooping at it with her hands so that spray rose to her left and right like shimmering, phantasmal wings. As she reached shallower water, she raised each leg to the side in turn to wrench it clear of the sea as if she were jumping hurdles, splashing through the breaking waves in an uncoordinated, knock-kneed run. "Sky!" she called. "Sky!"

Skydancer unfurled his wings

and leapt from his rock to land in the shallows, his head thrust toward Cara. She used his reins to haul herself to his shoulder and scramble up into the saddle.

"Go, Sky!" she cried. "Cut them off!"

Water fountained all around them as the dragon hurtled skyward, bugling a challenge. Cara buckled her safety belt and tether as she flew. She didn't feel the cold as the water evaporated from her clothes in the rush of their flight; all she could think of was catching up with her hated rival and stopping her from marauding Ronan's flock, at all costs.

Hortense led her wing in a long sweep seaward before turning back toward the land in order to herd the capricorns into the shallow waters of the bay. *She's done this before,* thought Cara with a surge of revulsion. But the maneuver also gave Cara time to intercept the Clapperclaw party. As she flew toward them she could hear their excited cries.

"There they are!"

"I bagsie a nice fat one!"

"Tally-ho!" The hunting cry was followed by a chorus of girlish cries and shrieks of laughter. Cara scowled. *They think it's fun,* she thought. *It's just a silly game to them.*

Intent on their prey, the hunting party had not spotted the dragon and rider rising to meet them. It came as quite a shock to Hortense when, as she prepared to swoop down on the panic-stricken capricorns, she suddenly found herself confronted by an angry dragon with a rider whose

clinging, salt-stained clothes, wild hair, and burning eyes made her look more like a banshee from Bresalian legend than anything human.

Hortense hurriedly reined in her dragon; her companions, equally bewildered, did likewise.

Then, realizing who it was that opposed her, Hortense twisted her face into a sneer. "Cara! Get of my way, you lunatic!"

"No!" Cara cried. "If you want to hunt the capricorns, you'll have to get past me first!"

Hortense said a very rude word, turned her dragon's head, and attempted to fly around Cara. But Cara had been expecting this, and so had Skydancer. He sideslipped to maintain his position in front of Hortense's mount. Hortense tried twice more to evade him, without success. No matter how quickly she tried to turn, Silvercloud was no match for Sky. Turning away in frustration, the High Lord's daughter signaled to the riders flying to her left and right.

Even with flying goggles masking half their faces, Cara thought she recognized them as cronies of Hortense's, younger riders from her father's private stables who were in their first year as Intermediate competitors. They were usually to be found wherever Hortense happened to be holding court, flattering her vanity and laughing at her jokes.

In obedience to Hortense's signal, they exchanged glances, then headed straight for Cara.

Cara calmly awaited their arrival. The dragons— a Firecrest and a Finback—flew at her with intimidating speed; then, at the last moment, they backed their wind and reared. Each belched out a gout of fiery breath in challenge.

Cara was taken aback. Dragons used their flame to show each other who was boss, but they weren't supposed to do it against dragons with human riders.

The dragons flared again. Cara's eyes narrowed. *Oho,* she thought, *you want to play rough, do you?*

While the riders were momentarily blinded by their own dragons' fire, Cara flew between them, feeling the heat of the flames. She pulled hard on the reins to bring her dragon up in a tight loop. "Show them, Sky!"

The movement had been too quick for the younger riders to follow. They stared around them with a consternation that was almost comical as they searched for the dragon that had suddenly disappeared before their very eyes. Then Skydancer, completing his loop, was once more before them and opening his mouth to flame.

There was a roar, a burst of heat, and a blinding flash of light. The two dragonriders cried out and threw their hands over their faces. Their dragons squealed and reared in terror, trying with frantic wing beats to back away from the searing flame. Then, as one, they dived down and fled.

Cara smiled grimly. They should have known better than to tangle with Skydancer: No dragon could flame like a Goldenbrow.

She flew serenely between the hunters and their would-be prey, watching with interest as Hortense signaled the fourth rider to fly to the attack. The rider shook her head. Hortense gestured again, more forcefully this time, to be met by the same response. They held a shouted conversation, too far away for Cara to hear.

Then Hortense turned back to Cara. With an angry gesture, she flung her arm out to the side with her palm flat and her thumb tucked beneath—the dragonriders' sign for talk—and pointed to the beach.

Cara also pointed to show agreement, but then pressed her hand against her chest and pointed again, meaning, "You lead, I'll follow." With a glare, Hortense jerked at her dragon's reins and headed for the beach. Her friends did likewise.

As soon as Skydancer touched down, Cara leapt from his back and strode toward Hortense, who remained on dragonback and scowled at her.

"Get lost, Hortense."

"Your manners," sneered Hortense, "are as delightful as ever."

"You've no business here," Cara told her fiercely. "Merfolk Bay isn't part of Clapperclaw's hunting range."

"We're not after any of the scrawny beasts from your worthless moors, Cara of Dragonsdale. The sea is everyone's hunting range." Hortense turned to her friends for confirmation. The younger riders twittered indignantly.

"That's right, Hortense."

"You tell her, Hortense."

The fourth rider said nothing. Looking at her closely for the first time, Cara recognized Ernestina. The Clapperclaw rider returned Cara's stare with her usual air of cool detachment.

Hortense resumed her attack. "You've no right to come between us and our prey."

"I've every right," said Cara, "when the prey belongs to someone else."

Hortense stared at her. "Those goat-fish? And to whom, pray tell, do they belong?"

"They're capricorns, and they belong to Ronan."

"And who might Ronan be?" scoffed Hortense. "Some horny-handed fisherlad you've taken a fancy to?"

"They belong," Cara told her slowly and clearly, "to Ronan of the merfolk."

"The merfolk?" Hortense was momentarily taken aback. Then she gave a howl of laughter. "Oh, that's priceless! Just when I thought you couldn't lower yourself any further, you go running—I beg your pardon, *swimming*—after a fish-tailed freak." Her two friends joined in with her laughter, barking like howlers.

Cara kept her temper with an effort. "The flock belongs to Ronan, and—"

"The flock?" crowed Hortense. Then her face hardened. "All right, Cara," she snapped. "The joke's over. Merfolk are savages. Barbarians. They have no flocks, no herds, and no rights. Those creatures are there to be hunted, and we're going to hunt them. Now, get out of my way."

"No."

"Hortense." Ernestina spoke for the first time. "We don't want any trouble. Perhaps we should find out what your father thinks before—"

Hortense rounded on her. "My father thinks the same as me!" A faint flush of color showed in Ernestina's cheeks, but she fell silent. "We have every right to hunt those beasts," Hortense insisted, "and she has no right to stop us."

"Right or wrong," said Cara quietly, "I will stop you."

"All four of us? I don't think so." Hortense's face twisted with rage. "For the last time—stand aside, fish-lover, or you'll be sorry."

Cara said nothing. She turned on her heel, walked back to Sky, and climbed into the saddle. Glowering, Hortense signaled her party to advance. Their dragons took one step forward . . . two . . . three . . .

Skydancer gazed at Hortense and her companions with eyes that smoldered like banked fires, needing only the merest stir to set them roaring once more. He rumbled deep in his throat. Then he flamed again.

The beach immediately in front of him was transformed instantly from sand into molten glass, which flowed briefly, then settled into wild wave shapes, cracking and bubbling as it cooled.

Cara patted Sky's neck.

He's getting good at that, she thought.

Whether or not Hortense and her younger friends would willingly have continued the confrontation, their dragons had had enough. Bugling with alarm, they rose like startled boobries, their wings practically whirring as they shot into the air. Heedless of their riders' frantic attempts to regain control, they sped over the cliffs, back the way they had come.

Only Ernestina and her dragon, Stormbringer, had not moved. The Clapperclaw rider eyed Cara steadily and touched her whip to her helmet in a respectful gesture that might or might not have been ironic. Then she urged her dragon into the air and set off to follow her companions.

Cara let out her breath in a great sigh of relief and slumped in her saddle. Sky craned his neck to look back at her and gave a concerned chirrup.

Cara rubbed the dragon's cheek and laughed shakily. "I'm fine, Sky, thanks for asking. How are you?"

Skydancer gave a soft hoot and swung his head away to point, like a hunting dog. Cara followed his gaze and saw a mane of dark hair bobbing in the waves, near an outcrop of rock that jutted into the sea.

Cara flicked the reins and Skydancer flew to the end of the rocks. She slipped from the saddle as the dragon furled his wings and settled into a crouch.

Ronan spluttered for a moment as though he really was in danger of drowning, apparently lost for words. "Your sky-dragon—that flame—amazing. So bright!" He raised himself from the water and bowed to Cara as he had done earlier to Skydancer. "I misjudged you, Cara. You stood alone against four enemies and saved my flock. Please accept my apologies."

Cara suddenly felt embarrassed and uneasy. "There's nothing to apologize for," she told Ronan. "Just please don't think all dragonriders are like Hortense."

"Now that I have met you, I know they are not." The merboy gave Cara a warm smile. "And I shall not forget." Without warning, he plunged beneath the surface, leaving hardly a ripple.

Cara leapt to her feet. "Wait! Will I see you again?"

But the only reply was the crying of the gulls and the lapping of the waves.

*   *   *

"Tell me what happened today, Cara."

Cara was standing on the faded carpet in her father's study. Dragonmaster Huw sat behind the heavy desk with its scuffed leather top, on which he wrote all the stable's records and accounts, and waited.

Taking a deep breath, Cara told him what had happened at Merfolk Bay. Huw steepled his fingers and listened carefully. When Cara had finished, he said, "Whatever the provocation, I cannot approve of dragonriders allowing their beasts to flame at each other."

"They started it, Da."

"Even so, no dragon should ever flame at a human. It is a violation of the Trustbond, Cara. You know that."

"Yes, but it was only a threat. No one got hurt."

The Dragonmaster's expression was stony. "Nevertheless."

Cara dropped her eyes. "Sorry, Da."

"Very well. Do not let it happen again."

"All right, Da," said Cara. "But I couldn't let them hunt Ronan's capricorns, could I?"

"There is a school of thought," Huw observed, "that would say that Hortense and her friends were acting entirely within their rights."

"But, Da . . ."

"I don't subscribe to that school," the Dragonmaster went on, ignoring the interruption, "but others do.

If Hortense's party had been hunting on our land, I would protest most vigorously—"

"So a Dragonsdale rabbit is worth more than a merfolk capricorn, is that it?"

Huw glared at his daughter. "If I may be allowed to finish?"

Cara said nothing.

"I was about to say that the sea is a gray area in the agreements between stables," Huw went on severely. "If I make a complaint, Lord Torin is bound to find against Dragonsdale—not only because his daughter is involved, or because relations between himself and Dragonsdale are currently strained, or even because he would anger the fisherfolk if he appeared to rule in favor of the merpeople—but because in Bresalian law there is actually no case for Hortense to answer."

"But she shouldn't be allowed to hunt the merpeople's flocks. It's wrong!"

"I agree with you," said Huw heavily, "and I sympathize with the merfolk. But I see no point in getting into a fight with Torin that I can't win, and damaging Dragonsdale without benefiting the people of the sea."

"But, Da . . . !"

"And let that be an end to the matter." Huw placed his elbows on the desk and leaned forward. "Now to another area of concern. I hear that you and Breena have been at loggerheads for some time."

Cara pouted. "It's not my fault! Breena—"

"I do not intend to be drawn into a foolish dispute between two riders, especially when one of them is my daughter." Huw's voice was uncompromising. "But I must tell you this. Personal jealousies and rivalries can be very dangerous, especially in formation flying. I did not want Mistress Hildebrand to recruit the two of you to the display team in the first place. I eventually agreed—not because she threatened to resign, though she did, several times"—Cara smiled wanly at this—"but because I agreed with her that flying together in a different kind of discipline from that demanded by the show ring might help Breena and Moonflight rebuild their Trustbond.

"But I began to regret my decision as soon as I realized how things now stand between you. I tell you frankly, Cara: If I had another two riders of the required standard with fit dragons, I would have already dropped both of you from the team." He tapped his index finger on the desk for emphasis. "Display riding requires absolute trust between riders. You know well enough that Dragonsdale's reputation rests partly on the performances of its display team. The livelihood of every one of us depends on that reputation, and I will not have it compromised. If you are to represent this stable at the Clapperclaw showing, I need your assurance that you and Breena will put this ridiculous feud behind you. Do I have it?"

In a low voice, Cara replied, "Yes, Da."

Huw held her gaze for a moment. Then he said, "Very well. That will be all."

Cara left the study with a dry mouth and a pounding heart. She had given her father the only answer she could. But patch up her quarrel with Breena? Just like that?

It was an easy thing to promise—but Cara suspected it would be a great deal harder to do.

A SHOCKING
DISPLAY

The rehearsals for the formation display were not going well.

The Dragonsdale team had been flying together for several seasons now, but two of its senior riders had retired. This, and Mistress Hildebrand's insistence that two more team members with a good chance of winning the All Bresal Championships should concentrate entirely on their competition flying, had deprived the team of its most experienced riders. The accident between Caley and Tomey had thrown everything still further out of kilter, and the arrival of Cara and Breena had done nothing to improve matters.

"I don't know what more I can do," said Mistress Hildebrand, watching with mounting exasperation as the team performed a barrel roll in a diamond formation that became increasingly ragged as the maneuver progressed. "I've given them the least prominent roles in the whole formation. I've simplified the flying routine. I've given them the breakaway pair maneuvers so they can practice apart from the rest of the team. The Clapperclaw showing is only a few days away, and they're still making no progress at all!"

"I'm sure you're doing your best, Hildebrand," said Huw. Galen gave a grunt that might have meant anything.

The Dragonmaster and his most senior staff members were watching the rehearsal from the practice ring. The formation team's maneuvers were arranged so that the most spectacular elements of the routine always took place above the arena, giving the crowd the best possible view.

At least, that was what was supposed to happen.

The team went into a climb in an arrow formation. Breena and Cara were supposed to be tucked in behind the team leader, forming the "shaft" of the "arrow." In fact, Moonflight was too

far behind the leader and off her line to the right, while Skydancer was too far to the left, so that the arrow looked as if its shaft was broken. Mistress Hildebrand shook her head and beat her riding whip against her boot.

At the rear of the formation, Cara gritted her teeth and urged Skydancer back into line. She was supposed to follow Breena in this maneuver, but Breena was in the wrong place (*Typical*, Cara thought angrily) and Cara was worrying so much about Breena's position that she'd forgotten to concentrate on her own.

At a hand signal from the team leader, Cara turned Skydancer to the left. As the team went into a loop, they slotted into position as the outermost dragon and rider in the V-shaped formation known as the goose skein. *I bet Breena hasn't remembered where she's supposed to go,* Cara thought. *Anyway, nobody can blame me if she hasn't.*

Now in its new formation, the team came over the top of its loop and headed earthward in a vertical dive. The dragons part-folded their wings for extra speed.

On the ground, Hildebrand crossed her fingers. "Better . . ."

"If they time this one wrong," said Galen dourly, "we'll be scraping them up off the ground for weeks."

Hildebrand gave him a furious glare. "Galen!"

"Just an observation."

But the team leader didn't get it wrong. The formation pulled out of its dive on the far side of the Dragonsbeck, which it crossed low enough to ruffle the reeds at the water's edge. Flying straight and level, the riders held their course until they were within a few dragonlengths of the practice ring. Then they pulled up, fanning out like an exploding firework. Most of the formation headed toward Dragonsdale House to regroup: Cara and Breena flew off to left and right to prepare for their opposition maneuvers.

Despite her promise to her father, Cara's relations with Breena were worse than ever. Being teammates had forced them to talk to each other, but most of that talk had taken the form of angry reproaches. Whenever flying maneuvers went wrong—which they did with monotonous regularity—the two riders would blame each other for the mistake and end up on even worse terms than before.

Their first maneuver was relatively simple. After the seven riders in the main wing had flown over the crowd in a swan formation, Breena and Cara had to come in from opposite sides of the arena and perform a bow to the crowd. The only difficulty lay in the slowness of the maneuver. The dragons had to hover; without the uplift provided by forward motion through the air, this was a tiring thing for them to do. As if this was not enough, they then had to tilt forward for the bow and then fly backward away from the arena—a most unnatural way of flying for a dragon, and one that they found very difficult.

In the practice round, Cara and Breena got their timing wrong. Cara arrived in position first and went

into a hover, then had to wait several seconds for Breena
to join her.

"Not getting you out of bed, are we?" she muttered
out of the side of her mouth as Breena and Moonflight
settled into position alongside her and Skydancer.

"You were too early," Breena snapped back.

"Early? You took so long, I thought Moony must be
laying an egg," said Cara nastily. Breena flushed.

They urged their dragons to bow and withdraw. Just
before they parted, Breena hissed, "Do you think you
could possibly get the timing right on the next one?"

"Never mind my timing," Cara told her hotly. "Worry
about your own."

The next maneuver for the two girls was an opposition
half-loop. They were supposed to fly in from either side
of the arena and cross as close to the center as possible,
then cross again at the top of the loop before rolling out
and flying back the way they had come. The move was a
shambles. This time, Breena arrived over the arena first so
that Cara passed underneath her as she climbed. Instead
of crossing again at the top of the loop, they passed each
other before Cara had completed her climb, and some
way from the arena.

Mistress Hildebrand closed her eyes and groaned.

The rest of the rehearsal went no better. By the time
the team came in to land and the ground crew stepped
forward to take their dragons' reins, nerves were jangled
and tempers frayed.

Cara leapt from her saddle and stormed across to Breena. "What do you think you're doing? You're flying like a novice with two left hands!"

"Oh! Novice, is it?" cried Breena. "What about you? You were so late on that opposition roll, I could have eaten my dinner while I was waiting, so, with cheese and biscuits for dessert!"

"Watch what you're doing in the Finglassian Death Roll. If you come that close again—"

"That will do!"

The furious girls pulled apart, glaring at each other, as the Dragonmaster, Galen, and Mistress Hildebrand strode toward them. Hildebrand looked as if she might emulate a dragon and start breathing fire at any moment. "I have never in my life seen such an inept performance," she raged as the riders looked sheepishly down and fidgeted with their flying helmets. She pointed her whip at Cara and Breena in turn. "You two in particular—words fail me."

"I shall cancel our appearance at Clapperclaw," said Huw. There were groans from some of the team, which a sharp glance from the Dragonmaster instantly quelled. "I shall plead injuries to the team. I would rather face the embarrassment of cancellation than the humiliation of a poor display. You clearly need more practice; whether you fly at the Dragonsdale showing will depend on your progress between now and then." He and Hildebrand strode off toward Dragonsdale House.

Looking pointedly at Breena, Galen said, "If a rider can't keep her place in a display formation, how can she expect to ride in the guard flight?" With a nod to the disconsolate team leader, he turned to follow the Dragonmaster.

Cara glanced at Breena. Her face was contorted by an expression of utter fury.

"That was your fault!" she raged at Cara. Sobbing with humiliation, she ran from the field.

"Don't blame me!" Cara called after her. "See if I care, anyway!"

But nobody saw Cara or Breena for the rest of the day. And late into the night, the sharp-eared lookout in the Dragonsdale guard tower could hear the sounds of anguished weeping from two stables at opposite ends of the yard: that of Moonflight, and that of Skydancer.

The Clapperclaw showing was the least popular of the year for the Dragonsdale riders. Not only did they and their dragons face a wearisome journey across Clonmoor, around the jagged peaks of Cloudside, and over the barren landscape of Clapperclaw Heights, but when they arrived at the rival farm, they knew they could not expect a cheery welcome.

Despite the fact that it was late summer, the skies above Clapperclaw were grim and threatening. Dank mists roiled in the valley bottoms, their vapors soaking the rocks and wiry grasses before collecting in oily pools stained brown with peat. The black-granite buildings of the stables did nothing to provide a homely contrast to the desolate landscape: Rather, the house and stables seemed to grow out of the bleak crags on which they stood, brooding over the training areas spread out on the valley floor below. The turrets and pointed arches of Clapperclaw House reached like gnarled, clutching fingers into the raw, gray sky. Grotesque dragon gargoyles adorned the walls beneath its gray-slated roof, and black wrought-iron fences marked out the farm's boundaries, as if warning away all unwelcome visitors. In every respect, the atmosphere around Clapperclaw was the complete opposite of Dragonsdale's friendly and welcoming air.

The showing was to take place in the valley, where a village of recently erected crimson-and-black tents did little to brighten the gloomy atmosphere. Traditionally, Clapperclaw dragons did very well at their home events—possibly because the depressing surroundings seemed to drain the life out of the other competitors, or possibly for other, darker reasons. It was whispered that Clapperclaw employed "unsporting" practices, though no one had ever found conclusive evidence to support this widely held view. ("I know they darn well cheat!" was Mistress Hildebrand's private comment on the matter. "I just wish I knew how they did it!")

The journey had been long and fractious. Breena and Cara had pointedly flown well away from each other, and the display team was still smarting from the fact that they were not allowed to perform at the showing. To make matters worse, when they arrived at Clapperclaw, the Dragonsdale riders were ordered to fly in a holding pattern and await permission to land.

I bet the Clapperclaw crew are doing this on purpose to tire us out, thought Cara. *As if we're not tired enough already!*

She guided Skydancer into a gentle turn, taking the opportunity to inspect the competition arena and make a mental note of the positions of the pylons and tall black masts, rigged out with obstacles of varying difficulty. "Looks tricky, Sky," she told the dragon. "We're going to have to be on best form if we're going to win a fourth gold rosette." But even Cara's excitement at this prospect

was dampened by a feeling of unease, and she shivered.

Eventually the Dragonsdale riders received the all-clear from a marshal stationed in one of Clapperclaw's taller turrets, and they swooped down in tight formation, heading for the paddock. The dragons landed in quick succession, and their riders dismounted. Without acknowledging each other, Breena and Cara positioned themselves at opposite ends of the large paddock and began to prepare Moonflight and Skydancer for the Intermediate Clear.

As Cara reached into a leather saddlebag and pulled out a brace of moorcocks for Sky to munch on, Drane appeared at her side. "How was your journey?" he asked.

"Windy, wet, and long," replied Cara. "But I enjoy riding Skydancer in any weather." She held out the moorcocks, which were snatched out of her hand by the hungry dragon and quickly devoured. "It's just a shame we had to end up here. It's a bit bleak. What about your journey?"

"Terrible!" moaned Drane. "I was thrown around in a calash for hours. I was freezing cold, and I get so airsick. I nearly threw up when we were coming in to land."

"Shame you didn't," Cara told him. "We could do with a splash of color around here."

"Thank you very much." Drane eyed his surroundings with disfavor. "If I had my way, I wouldn't be here at all." Cara said nothing. Drane had every reason to dislike Clapperclaw; its guard flight had failed to help when firedogs and howlers had raided his family's farm. "But Mistress Hildebrand said I should go and offer my services to Dragonmaster Adair," Drane went on, "so I did."

"What job have you been given this time? Squirrelman or ring-rat?"

"Neither. He said that he had all the experienced people he needed. Makes you think, doesn't it?" Drane nodded toward the ring, where all the riggers, squirrelmen, and ring-rats were dressed in the crimson of Clapperclaw. "It's the only stable where they use only their own people to run the ring, and according to Mistress Hildebrand their riders always do well here. . . ." He left the implication hanging in the air.

"The ground crew can't do anything if I fly clear." Cara laughed. "So that's what I'll have to do!"

Drane smiled. "You're going for another win, then?"

"Fingers crossed." She patted Sky's neck. "After all, I've got the best dragon in the whole of Bresal. You're wonderful, aren't you?"

Sky stretched his neck and gave a hoot as if to say, "Of course I am!"

There was a pause as Drane peered down the paddock. "How's Breena?" he asked.

Cara's demeanor changed in an instant. "Ask her yourself," she snapped.

Drane sighed. "Cara, isn't it time you two made up?"

"I don't have anything to make up—and I don't see what it's got to do with you, anyway."

Drane's face clouded. "I may be just a stable hand, a go-and-get-it, a pair of hands to be dirtied, but even I know that friends are hard to make and easy to lose." His voice was somber. "And I also know that you don't realize the true value of something until it's gone and lost forever." With that, he turned on his heel and headed off.

"Oh, what does he know, Sky?"

Skydancer remained quiet as Cara reached into her grooming bag for a buffer brush and began to rub hard at his scales.

"He's just a boy." Cara was still smarting from Drane's parting words. "He doesn't know what it's like to ride a dragon, and he certainly doesn't know how it feels to win a competition." She spat on the buffer and scrubbed at a stubborn mark. "It's not my fault if Breena hasn't qualified for the championships, is it? And it's not my problem, either—it's hers."

But a small thought still nagged at her: Even if it wasn't her problem, could she be part of the solution? Maybe Drane was right after all. Maybe it was time to make up. If she could only find some way to reach out to Breena, to show her that they could be friends again . . .

"Cara of Dragonsdale?"

Cara turned to see a small, black-haired girl dressed in a crimson riding jacket. "That's me," she replied.

"I've been told to tell you that Wony wants to see you. She's waiting for you by the refreshment tent near the novices' ring." Without waiting for a reply, the girl hurried away.

"Wony!" exclaimed Cara guiltily. "I'd forgotten about her. I wonder how she and Bumble coped with the journey."

Wony and Bumble had set off for Clapperclaw just after dawn. Mistress Hildebrand and several members of the guard flight had escorted the Dragonsdale beginners and novices across the island in order to make sure that riders and dragons were in a fit state to compete at the showing and, more important, to ensure that no rider went missing.

"I wonder what she wants." Cara picked at a piece of leaf trapped between Sky's scales. The dragon swung his head from side to side. "She may need some advice . . . or money to buy a cake or two, more likely," she added, laughing to herself. She patted Skydancer's neck. "You'll be fine here, Sky. I won't be long, and there's still plenty of time to get you ready for the competition." Cara made sure that her dragon was tethered securely and made her way through the gathering crowd of spectators.

But when she arrived at the large pudding-shaped refreshment tent, there was no sign of Wony. Cara stood waiting at the entrance, glancing around and wondering where her young friend was. As the minutes passed, she

began to lose patience. "Come on, Wony," she muttered.
"I haven't got all day!" She was just about to return to Sky
when a voice from inside the tent brought her up sharp.

"I just don't understand Cara."

Cara went cold. The voice was Hortense's.

ONE MISTAKE
TOO MANY

Cara risked a peep around the tent flap. At a table just inside the entrance, the High Lord's daughter was tucking into a cream tea with one of the hangers-on who had been with her when Cara had interrupted their hunting at Merfolk Bay. Cara jerked her head back out of sight and listened intently.

"Cara?" The hanger-on's voice was muffled; she was obviously speaking with her mouth full. "What do you mean?"

"Treating her so-called friend in such a beastly manner. It's really upset Breena," said Hortense. "She's spoken to me about it."

Cara gave a little cry and quickly clapped her hand over her mouth. Breena and Hortense? Speaking about her?

"She can't understand what Cara is playing at." Hortense sounded quite at a loss. "And neither can anyone else. Everyone is talking about the situation. Breena's in tears practically every day—not that she'd let Cara see, but everyone else knows how unhappy she is. She so badly wants to ride in Dragonsdale's guard flight, but she won't be allowed to unless she qualifies for the championships, and everyone is saying that Cara isn't supporting her at all. If anything, she's doing the opposite. . . ."

Cara flushed with embarrassment. Was that what everyone thought? That she was being unfair to Breena?

On the other side of the tent wall, Hortense continued. "I can't believe Cara is being so selfish. I know that no one since her mother has won every Clear Flight in a season, and yes, it would be a wonderful achievement if Cara could do the same . . . but there are more important things in life." Hortense's voice took on a self-righteous tone. "Friends matter more than rosettes."

"Oh, Hortense, that is so true!"

"You'd think that Cara would ease off and instead help Breena qualify for the Island Championships. I mean, she's already qualified three times over! And it's Breena's last chance in the intermediates. What does winning another rosette matter, compared to friendship?"

"You're absolutely right, Hortense." The other girl's voice dripped with flattery.

"If I was in the same position as Breena, you'd do that for me, Jemima, wouldn't you?"

"Of course! Friends come first."

"Not in Cara's case. *She* wants to come first—all the time."

Outside the tent, Cara remembered Breena's words after the race home and felt ashamed.

"Well, maybe she was never Breena's real friend," continued Hortense. "Cara just used her when she wasn't allowed to ride, and now that she is riding, she's treating Breena like you'd treat dragon dung on a riding boot!"

Cara felt wretched. Was Breena really that unhappy? Was she, Cara, really being that selfish? The questions were quickly followed by memories of happy times shared with Breena: grooming and mucking out the dragons, picnics by the sea, weighing dragonets, laughing together, crying together, helping each other, and being . . . well . . . being friends. Cara's stomach knotted, and she felt sick. Friends were more important than rosettes. She *was* being selfish!

I have to do something, Cara thought. *I have to do what a friend should do.* She turned on her heel and hurried away.

She didn't see Hortense and her friend stepping from out of the refreshment tent to watch her go, grinning like howlers. Nor did she see Hortense mouthing "Well done!" and handing over a silver penny to a small, black-haired girl dressed in a crimson riding jacket.

The day continued, overcast and gloomy. Black clouds bruised the sky and dampened the spirits of the spectators.

In the paddock, Cara set about grooming Sky. But as her hands worked at polishing the dragon's scales and picking mud from his claws, her mind was elsewhere. She was thinking about how she could put things right with Breena, and was oblivious to the hubbub around her as anxious parents clucked and fussed over their children like mother hens.

"Livinia, how many times do I have to tell you? It should be a double plait, not a single!"

"I told you not to have that third cake before you rode! You can clean that mess off your jacket yourself!"

"Think hands, think posture, just think!"

Eventually Sky was in prime condition, but Cara hadn't the heart to enter him for the Intermediate Best Presented (which was won by Hortense, to no one's surprise). But by the time the flying competition started, she had formulated a plan to help Breena qualify for the Island Championships.

As the bell rang out across the arena to signal the beginning of the Intermediate Clear Flight, Cara looked down the length of the paddock. Breena was leading Moonflight. Mistress Hildebrand was walking alongside her, no doubt passing on words of advice and encouragement.

With a look of fierce determination on her face, Cara put on her helmet and mounted Skydancer. She settled herself into the saddle, but before strapping herself in, she leaned forward, holding the dragon's great muscled neck to steady herself. "We can't tell anyone about this, Sky.

I know you love winning, and so do I, but there are some things that are more important. What we're going to do is . . ." She moved even farther forward and whispered in the dragon's ear.

The bell sounded again, and the Intermediate Clear Flight competition began. Cara urged Skydancer forward and the dragon pounded toward the ring entrance, where Cara pulled him to a stop to watch the early competitors and await her turn.

The first few riders posed little or no threat; dragons from Drakelodge and Wyvernwood hit obstacles with a regularity that the suspicious in the crowd might have put down to Clapperclaw skulduggery, but which to Cara's eyes was due more to incompetent riding. *That's good for Breena,* she thought, smiling as she watched the ring-rats scurrying to retrieve the fallen poles and rods. *The more obstacles down, the better her chances of winning a rosette and qualifying.*

As riders came and went, the performances improved. Nevertheless, no one managed to fly clear; the course was proving a tricky one for all riders. Even with the home advantage, Hortense performed miserably as usual, but Cara noted that she didn't seem unduly bothered by this, which was puzzling.

By the time Cara and Skydancer were due to fly, three riders were on ten penalties.

Then it was her turn to take to the ring. The announcer's voice echoed across the arena: "The next competitor in the Intermediate Clear Flight is Cara of Dragonsdale, attempting to win her fourth consecutive gold rosette."

"Here we go, Sky." Cara urged the dragon forward. With a single flap of his great wings, Skydancer took to the air and flew into the ring.

After a couple of quick circuits to familiarize herself with the course, Cara turned Sky around and headed toward the first obstacle, a simple double horizontal with enough space for even the most cautious riders to guide their dragons through.

"This is for Breena," whispered Cara.

The dragon flew toward the middle of the gap, but at the last second, Cara gave a flick on her leg reins, causing Sky to dip down. As he glided through the obstacle, his belly touched the bottom pole and dislodged it.

There was a gasp of surprise from the crowd. Even the Clapperclaw squirrelman watching from high on the nearest mast looked incredulous. Cara of Dragonsdale, winner of three consecutive gold rosettes, had hit the first obstacle! Ten penalties! There would be no clear flight—was this the end of her winning run?

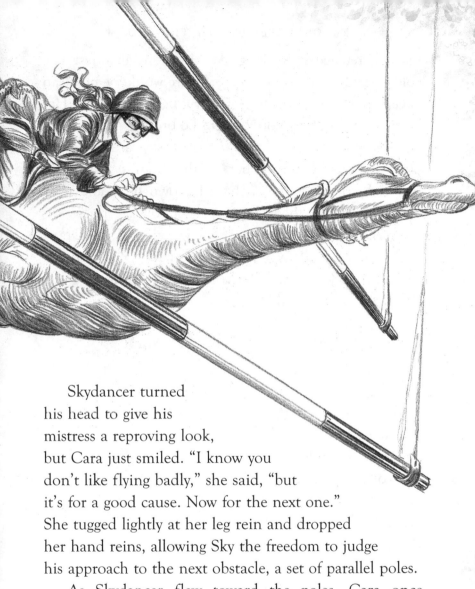

Skydancer turned
his head to give his
mistress a reproving look,
but Cara just smiled. "I know you
don't like flying badly," she said, "but
it's for a good cause. Now for the next one."
She tugged lightly at her leg rein and dropped
her hand reins, allowing Sky the freedom to judge
his approach to the next obstacle, a set of parallel poles.

As Skydancer flew toward the poles, Cara once
again gave an almost imperceptible flick of the reins.
Sky eased to his left, catching the right-hand pole with

his outstretched right wing. Another ten penalties! The gold rosette was definitely gone. There would be no clean sweep of the Intermediate Clear Flight for Cara. Her mother's record was not going to be broken.

Standing in the paddock, eyes skyward, Mistress Hildebrand scowled. "What in the Islands is the girl doing? Letting the dragon have his own head and then correcting him at the last minute. Schoolgirl error!"

Watching amid a group of fellow stable hands, Drane was also bemused by Cara's performance. "It must be the Clapperclaw crew—they've done something to Sky," he told all who would listen.

And it was all that Hortense could do to stop herself from laughing outright.

Like Hortense, but for very different reasons, Cara was happy. She sent Sky into a steep dive before straightening up and flying him parallel to the ground, heading toward a set of slalom poles. Instead of flicking his body around each of the wands, at Cara's command Sky straightened up and hit every single pole—*Whack! Whack! Whack! Whack! Whack!* The poles spun into the air, causing the ring-rats to dive for cover as they rained down on them. Fifty more penalties!

"That's enough," Cara told Sky. "Now let's show them what you *really* can do. . . ."

The rest of the round went by in a flash. There were no more obstacles hit, no more penalties lost. Sky and

Cara flew beautifully together. Poles, hoops, and rods were cleared with room to spare and they completed the round to a smattering of sympathetic but bemused applause.

"Why didn't she fly like that throughout?" muttered Mistress Hildebrand. "Wretched girl. Seventy penalty points, indeed."

Cara flew through the gate and landed facing Breena, who was next to go. Cara shrugged and gave a rueful grin, but Breena made no response. Her face might have been carved out of stone. She opened her mouth to say something, but at that moment the bell rang to summon her to the arena, and she turned away and flicked the reins, signaling Moonflight to take off.

Cara stared after her. Now what had she done?

She had no time to consider the matter further. Mistress Hildebrand was striding across the paddock toward her, scowling ferociously. "What in the Isles were you playing at?" she demanded. "I've never witnessed such a piece of incompetent dragonriding. And I've seen some in my time, let me tell you!"

"Sorry," said Cara. "I don't know what happened," she lied, crossing her fingers behind her back.

"A chance to go for the record! Gone! It might never happen again."

"Friends matter more than rosettes, Mistress Hildebrand."

"What's that supposed to mean?"

"Just something I heard," replied Cara.

Mistress Hildebrand fixed her with a narrow-eyed stare. "So that's the way of it?" She gave her head a weary shake. "Don't believe everything you hear, my girl." She tapped her riding boot with her whip. "Well, what's done is done. Let's hope your friend manages to profit from your 'mistakes.'" The riding instructor stomped away.

"My friend," repeated Cara. "Yes, let's hope she does." Hurriedly she tethered Sky, giving him another moorcock to soothe his injured pride. Then she raced to the arena, arriving just as Breena began her round.

Moonflight started well, dealing easily with the first three obstacles. Even the narrow parallel poles presented no problems. Looking on, tight-chested and nervous, Cara could hardly breathe. With only a handful of competitors to go, if Breena flew clear she would probably win. Even ten penalties would practically guarantee her a place in the fly-off. "Come on, Breena, you can do it," she whispered.

In the air, however, Breena was not so confident. Despite her outward appearance of calm, she could feel Moonflight's hesitancy. She couldn't give her dragon a loose rein and trust her to tackle the obstacles bravely. Their Trustbond, though not severed, was not wholly mended, either. A rider needed to be at peace with herself if she was to be at one with her dragon, and the events of the previous months meant that Breena was in a state of conflict and turmoil.

But she was also set on qualifying for the championships. With her natural flying skills and through dogged determination, Breena cajoled Moonflight around the course. They were still clear as they came to the final three obstacles.

On the ground, Cara was flying with Breena, mirroring every move she made, clutching at imaginary reins, shifting her body position, and willing her friend to fly clear and win a rosette.

Approaching a triple set of horizontals, Breena pulled back on her reins. "Easy, Moony, easy," she commanded. The dragon slowed down to take the first part of the obstacle, but then seemed to panic and flicked her tail, hitting the second pole and dislodging it. Ten penalties!

Cara groaned. "Come on, Breena, you can still do it! You can still make the fly-off!"

High above Cara, Breena gritted her teeth. "No more!" she hissed. "No more!" She turned Moonflight around and flew toward the penultimate obstacle, a small hoop, which needed to be taken at speed in order to bring the dragon into position for the narrow horizontal.

Like Cara, the spectators were caught up in the drama of the situation. All eyes looked skyward as Breena kicked on. Moonflight responded to her rider and

increased her speed. At the last moment, she tucked in her wings and flew clear through the hoop.

"Yes!" Cara punched the air. "Come on, Breena, come on. Just clear the last!"

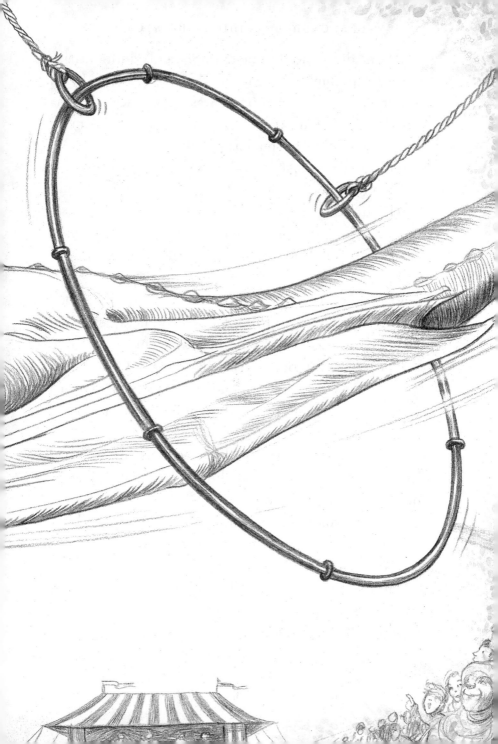

Breena didn't need to be told. She pulled Moonflight into a steep climb, heading for the last obstacle. In an instant, the narrow horizontal was upon them. Breena tucked herself tightly into the saddle, trying to make herself and Moony as small as possible.

The dragon shot toward the gap.

Cara held her breath.

The crowd stared, openmouthed.

And then, just as it seemed that all was going to work out for the best, Moonflight's back leg nudged against the bottom rod.

Cara looked on in horror as the rod shook uncontrollably, seemed to settle for a moment, and then came out of its sling and plummeted down.

The crowd let out a collective groan. Cara closed her eyes. Twenty penalties. Breena had failed to reach the fly-off. She still had not qualified for the Island Championships.

Cara hurried to the paddock, where Breena had landed and was already unsaddling Moonflight. "Breena," she began, "I'm so sorry. . . ."

Breena swung around on Cara. Her face was livid. "What exactly did you think you were doing up there?"

Cara took a step back. "What?"

"You never fly that badly! Don't think I don't know what you were up to. You hit those obstacles deliberately. I saw you! You were trying to lose!"

Cara was nonplussed. "Well—all right, yes, I was—but I did it—"

"I know why you did it—to give me a chance. How dare you?" Breena was barely in control of herself. "Listen to me, Cara of Dragonsdale—the day I need your help to win a competition, I'll give up dragonriding altogether."

Cara felt her cheeks burning. "But—I only thought . . ."

"You only thought you'd rub my face in it still further by proving that I could only beat you if you allowed me to? Thanks for nothing! Don't you ever humiliate me like that again!"

Rage boiled up in Cara. She'd thrown away her chance to equal her mother's achievement in order to help Breena, only to have her generosity thrown back in her face. "I wasn't trying to humiliate you, I was trying to help you. And I wouldn't have needed to do it if you and Moonflight weren't so completely useless!"

The second the words were out, Cara wished she could take them back. But they could not be unsaid. Cara and Breena stared at each other, aghast, chillingly aware that a boundary had been crossed from which there could be no going back.

Into the cold silence, a voice intruded. "Cara, Breena. Look! A green rosette! We won it, Bumble and me! Our first-ever rosette for flying. Look!"

Cara tore her eyes away from Breena's as Wony, her face wreathed in smiles, came running across the paddock with Drane at her heels. Beaming, she held up her rosette.

In a harsh voice, Cara said, "Not now, Wony."

Wony looked from Cara to Breena and back again, suddenly aware of the animosity between them. Her face crumpled. The green rosette fell from her hand.

Breena flashed Cara a look of pure loathing and led Moonflight away. Cara glared at her retreating back. "Of all the ungrateful—"

"Why don't you shut up!"

Shocked, Cara turned to face Drane. His eyes were glinting and his mouth was set in a tight, thin line.

"Just for once," he said harshly, "it would be nice if you and Breena tried thinking about someone besides yourselves." He turned his back on Cara and picked up Wony's dropped rosette. "Come on, Wony," he said. "Let's go and show this to Mistress Hildebrand. I'm sure she'll be interested."

"Wony . . ." Cara pulled herself together with an effort and took a deep breath. "Look, I'm sorry—I meant to say, 'Well done.' Green, ay? That's really . . . really . . ."

"Don't overdo it, will you?" said Drane with heavy sarcasm.

Cara turned on him. "Leave me alone, Drane. Can't you see I'm upset?"

"Oh, *you're* upset? Too bad for you. Of course, while you and Breena are behaving like a couple of spoiled brats, it's all right if you upset everybody else in the bargain."

Cara stamped her foot. "Why don't you mind your own business?" She turned on her heel and stormed off.

Drane ignored her. "And after we've seen Mistress Hildebrand," he said to Wony, "how about a big slice of cake?"

Wony brightened a little.

"Cherry sponge cake?"

Wony's eyes twinkled.

"With spoonfuls of cream filling?"

Wony nodded eagerly.

"Let's go and find some."

Hortense practically skipped across the grass to the Clapperclaw picket lines, humming a merry tune.

Ernestina had taken off her showing jacket; it hung on the wattle fence of Stormbringer's enclosure, the gold rosette on the lapel glinting in the sun. She looked up at Hortense's approach. "You're in a good mood."

Hortense gave a self-satisfied grin. "Cara and Breena have just had the most frightful row!"

Ernestina went back to rubbing down her dragon. "Have they?" she said indifferently.

"Yes—and, though I say it myself, I really think I deserve a lot of the credit."

Ernestina carried on wiping dust and dirt from Stormbringer's scales.

Hortense lounged against the wall of the enclosure, idly flicking her riding whip. "Yes—no one can say I don't look after my friends. Even the ones who won't back me up when a certain nuisance from Dragonsdale stops me from going after prey I'm perfectly entitled to hunt." She gave her friend an accusing look, to which Ernestina, to all appearances, remained oblivious. Hortense sniffed. "Oh, don't bother to thank me. You're perfectly welcome."

Ernestina rubbed hard at a patch of scales that looked quite clean already. "Thank you for what?"

"For getting you your first win of the season."

Ernestina froze.

Hortense prattled on. "I must say, it was rather brilliant of me. I made Cara think that if she was really Breena's friend, she'd let her win. So Cara flew badly on purpose, and then, of course, Breena didn't win—she's flying like a wyvern with hiccups, so that was never going to happen—and that left the field wide open for you."

To Hortense's surprise, Ernestina seemed less than delighted by the news that her victory had only come about through Hortense's interference.

"What's the matter?" she demanded. "Aren't you pleased?"

Ernestina said nothing. She went back to her rubbing.

Hortense glared at her. "Oh, that's charming! I do someone a good turn, and what thanks do I get?" She stalked off, nose in the air.

Ernestina straightened up and rubbed her hands on the cloth, lost in thought. Dropping the rag into a bucket, she crossed the enclosure and reached for her showing jacket. She unpinned the gold rosette and stood quite still for a moment, looking at it and feeling the soft ribbon between her fingers.

Then she slipped the rosette into her equipment bag and fastened the flap so that she couldn't see it anymore.

DEATH ROLL

Cara swam in the clear, cold waters of Merfolk Bay. Skydancer lay curled up on a rock at the sea's edge, snoozing and basking in the late-afternoon sun.

Since the Clapperclaw showing, Breena had maintained her angry silence. Even Moonflight seemed to share her mistress's view of Cara, snorting and flapping her wings whenever she caught sight of her. Perhaps for this reason, Moonflight and Breena were flying better together. It was as if their dislike of Cara was strengthening their Trustbond. This resulted in much better practices for Breena, with fewer obstacles knocked down, but did nothing to make Cara feel less lonely and unloved, especially since Drane and Wony had not forgiven her and were also maintaining their distance.

Even the formation practices were going better now that Breena and Cara had stopped sniping at each other. Instead, they ignored each other completely, and listened only to the team leader, who had learned to keep his dealings with both girls as businesslike as possible and not to praise or blame either at the expense of the other. Thus, a fragile truce was established, and performances improved to the point where Mistress Hildebrand stopped threatening to resign after every practice and Huw grudgingly agreed that the team could perform at the Dragonsdale showing, the last of the season.

In her free time, Cara had taken to flying Skydancer to Merfolk Bay to revisit the scene of her meeting with Ronan. She hoped each time that she would see the merboy again, but she never had.

Cara flipped onto her back and floated, rocked by gentle waves, staring up into the cloudless sky. It was

all so peaceful.
Lying here like
this, she could
forget all her
worries, all the
misery of falling
out with Breena;
she could lie here
like this forever. . . .

"Cara."

Startled by the voice
in her ear, Cara gasped, and
completely forgot to swim. Her head
dipped below the waves. Salty water stung
her eyes and shot up her nose. Coughing
and spluttering, she fought her way back to the
surface—and found herself staring into a familiar
grinning face.

"Ronan!"

Skydancer hooted a welcome.

The merboy looked around, as though checking that
he and Cara were not being observed. Then he let a wave
carry him onto the rocks below Skydancer and, with
perfect timing, hauled himself neatly up to sit at the
water's edge. He reached a hand out to Cara, who took
it and scrambled up to join him.

Ronan gave Cara a shy half smile. "I am glad to see you."

"I'm glad, too." Cara clambered over the rocks to
take an old piece of blanket from Sky's saddlebag and
vigorously rubbed at her hair. "Is your sea-dragon
with you?"

"Mordannsair?"

"Is that its name?"

"His name," said Ronan. "Yes, he's out there waiting
for me. He doesn't like to swim so close inshore." He

splashed at the water with his tail. A few moments later, the fantastic beast Cara had seen Ronan ride to protect his flock emerged from the sea, several dragonlengths out, and gave the strange bubbling cry she had heard before. Cara stared, entranced, and sighed as the beautiful creature sank back beneath the waves.

She spread the blanket on the rocks and sat on it. "I was beginning to think I'd never find you again," she said. "I've been here lots of times. . . ."

"I know. I have seen you."

"Then why didn't you come over and say hello?"

Ronan looked abashed. "Well—my people do not really understand. I told them what you did to save my capricorn, but they think I am making it up or exaggerating. I am afraid they do not really trust humans at all. They were angry that I had spoken to you, and they did not want me to see you again."

"I know what you mean." Ever since Cara had thwarted her attempt to hunt the capricorns, Hortense had been making snide remarks about Cara's fancying a merboy, and encouraging her friends to call her names, of which "fish-lover" was one of the mildest. Cara tried not to mind this; ordinarily she couldn't care less what any of Hortense's cronies thought of her. But since her own friends were hardly speaking to her, the insults had more effect than they otherwise would have. Cara could well understand Ronan's reluctance to meet her again, if he had been getting the same sort of treatment.

Ronan sighed. "My people are very set in their ways. It does not occur to them that different people can get on together. They have an old saying about meetings between merfolk and sky-dragon riders: Fire and water never can be friends."

"Fire and water," repeated Cara. She draped the blanket over her shoulders and sat down beside Ronan. "Well, I don't see why some stupid old saying should stop us from being friends if we want to be." She thrust her hand out.

Ronan looked taken aback—hand-shaking obviously wasn't a custom among the merfolk—but after a moment's thought he realized what Cara wanted him to do. Hesitantly, he took her hand and shook it. Cara had half expected his skin to feel cold and fishlike, and was agreeably surprised to find that it was as warm and human as her own.

Ronan let go of Cara's hand and turned away shyly. Cara gasped. "You're hurt!"

Ronan looked surprised. "No, I'm not. Where?"

"There are great cuts across your back—three of them, each side! Something must have bitten you—was it a shark?"

Ronan stared at her, openmouthed, for a moment. Then he laughed so hard he nearly fell off his rock.

"What's so funny?"

Eventually Ronan's mirth died down long enough to allow him to explain. "Those are my gills. I need them to breathe underwater. Out of the water, I use my lungs."

Cara stared, fascinated, at the fluttering flaps of skin covering the merboy's gill slits.

"Fish only have gills," Ronan told her proudly, "and porpoises, dolphins, and capricorns only have lungs. I have both, so I can breathe air longer than any fish and stay underwater longer even than a dolphin."

"I suppose," said Cara thoughtfully, "that swimming underwater must be like flying."

"Perhaps it is," said Ronan. "I would not know. I have never flown."

"I mean—when I'm flying with Sky, I'm up above everything. I see all the forests and streams and lakes below me, like another world. When I'm flying, I belong to the world of air, and when I'm not, I belong to the world of earth. . . ."

"And when your dragon flames, he belongs to the world of fire, too." There was yearning in Ronan's voice. "You are lucky, you dragonriders. You are masters of earth, air, and fire."

"And water, too," Cara reminded him. "Some of us can swim."

Ronan gave a bark of laughter. "No offense, Cara, but you swim like a flounder with fin-rot. And you can't swim underwater—you can only touch the surface of our world. Be happy with three elements. We have only one, water, yet within it we are free—free to wander through our kelp forests and sea caves, free to swim in the sunlit shallows or the deep waters where it is always dark."

"Then perhaps you are luckier than we are," said Cara. She looked up at Sky, who craned his neck so that she could stroke his eye ridges. "Without our dragons, we'd never be able to leave the earth." She fell silent; for the first time, she felt she understood exactly how much the Trustbond offered humans.

Then she shivered and looked to the west. "It's getting late," she said regretfully. "I have to go."

"So do I. But if you come here again, will you call me?"

"How do I do that?"

"Slap the water three times." Ronan flapped his flat tail flukes against the sea. The sound echoed off the cliffs like giant handclaps.

Cara clambered down to the water's edge. "Like this?" She patted at the water with the palm of her hand. The sound she produced was pathetic, nothing like the resounding slaps of Ronan's tail.

Ronan laughed. "No—I'll never hear that. . . ."

Slap! Slap! Slap!

Ronan and Cara turned and stared at Skydancer. Looking very pleased with himself, the dragon raised his tail and brought its spade end down on the surface of the sea with three more resounding slaps.

"Yes," said Ronan, grinning. "I think I shall hear that. Farewell, Cara. Farewell, friend sky-dragon."

And with that, he dived into the waves, barely making a splash, and was gone.

Over the following weeks there was little time for the animosity between Cara and Breena to develop further, as everyone at Dragonsdale worked hard to be ready for the final showing of the year. Dragonmaster Huw impressed on everyone the importance of maintaining the farm's reputation.

The practice ring was transformed into a show arena, tents were erected, and plans put into place for accommodating large numbers of spectators and competitors. All this activity took place on top of the usual life of the farm: Guard flights still had to be flown and training sessions undertaken, and mucking out was still a daily chore. Dragons and riders spent more time than usual practicing, and Mistress Hildebrand and the senior riders were in constant demand.

In the kitchen, Gerda and her team of helpers worked long hours ordering and receiving the huge amount of provisions needed. Bags and bags of flour, ground from recently harvested grain, arrived on a daily basis from the Dragonsbeck water mill. Orchards were stripped of apples and plums. Children were sent out to scour hedges for blackberries, sloes, and gooseberries, arriving back with bulging baskets of fruit and suspicious stains around their lips. Gerda, her face as red as the fires of her ovens, labored to transform these simple foodstuffs into delicious loaves of bread, fruit pies, and cakes. She prided herself on producing the very best refreshments of all the Seahaven showings; it was said that many people attended the Dragonsdale event not for the flying competitions but to sample Gerda's cooking.

As the showing approached, Breena and Moonflight were almost back to their best form. Cara was glad about this: It meant that it would be all the more satisfying to beat Breena, and after the events at Clapperclaw, Cara had no intention of holding back. She was quite happy for Breena to take second or third place and qualify for the Island Championships, if she could, but she fully intended that she and Skydancer were going to win.

The display team, too, was performing well, but tensions between the riders bubbled beneath the surface, ready to break out at any moment. The team was balanced on a knife edge.

As Cara saddled Skydancer for the formation display on the day of the showing, she wasn't particularly surprised to find Hortense watching her. "Did you want something?" she asked coldly.

"No . . . no." Hortense shook her head, but did not move away.

Cara carried on buckling straps until she became tired of being watched. "Look, if you've something to say, say it!"

"Well—it's just . . ." Hortense's voice was nervous and unhappy. "You won't take any silly risks, will you?" she blurted at last.

Cara stared at her. "What are you talking about?"

"Oh, dear, I'm not doing this very well. Look, I know we're not friends. . . ."

"You can say that again!"

"But even so, I don't want to see . . ." Hortense took a deep breath. "It's just that I was talking to Breena, and she said . . . well, you know the Finnglassian Death Roll, where you fly at each other from opposite ends of the arena and both turn at the last minute?"

"Yes, of course I do!"

"Well—she said you were pulling out of it too early . . ."

"Oh, she did, did she?"

". . . so everyone could see you were flying to miss each other and it didn't look convincing. I said you were only thinking of her safety, and she said . . . she said she knew whose safety you were thinking of, and it wasn't hers."

Cara jerked on a strap so hard that Skydancer gave her a reproachful look.

"Anyway, she said she was going to talk to you about it. Has she?"

"No," said Cara, gritting her teeth.

"Oh—oh, dear—then perhaps I shouldn't . . ."

Hortense's air of confusion was masterly. This wasn't entirely surprising, as she had already practiced it: She had had an almost identical conversation with Breena just a few minutes before.

"Well, I'm sorry if I . . . at any rate, I'm sure you'll be sensible." Hortense dithered for a moment, then departed from the scene, leaving Cara seething with fury. It wasn't that she believed what Hortense had said—well, not really—but she didn't entirely disbelieve it, either. And as she finished harnessing her dragon, Cara determined that if anyone pulled out of any moves early, it wouldn't be her and Skydancer.

The opening maneuvers of the Dragonsdale team's display went well. The diamond formation was tight, the shaft of the arrow was straight, and in the goose skein the formation was as accurate as if it had been drawn with a ruler. Then came the firework burst, and while the main flight headed toward Dragonsdale House to regroup, Cara and Breena brought their dragons over the arena, with perfect timing, to bow to the crowd.

As Skydancer and Moonflight labored to fly backward, Cara cast a glance at her fellow rider. Even with the current

lack of friendship between them, Cara was startled by the look of fixed enmity and scorn on Breena's face.

All right, then, she thought grimly. *We'll see whose nerve breaks first.*

The display continued with practiced efficiency until Cara and Breena flew out to begin the final maneuver of their routine. The Finnglassian Death Roll was a risky but spectacular stunt that never failed to bring a gasp from the crowd. All Cara and Breena had to do was fly straight at each other until, at the last minute, both would bank their dragons to the right to pass talon-to-talon, apparently avoiding a midair collision by a scalesbreadth, and complete the roll as they parted.

The secret was all in the timing.

Cara turned at the northwest pylon and sent Skydancer racing back toward the showing arena. At the southeast pylon, Breena did likewise. The crowd in the stands looked from left to right in growing expectation.

Cara's knees tightened against the saddle, and her hands gripped the reins so hard that the leather cut

into her flesh. Her teeth were bared in a ferocious scowl.
I won't break first, she thought, *I won't* . . .

The two dragons hurtled toward each other.

Cara held on as Moonflight loomed larger and larger
in her vision. Skydancer automatically began to bank, but
Cara controlled him with a flick of the reins. Not yet,
not yet . . .

Everything seemed to speed up and slow down all
at the same time. Skydancer and Moonflight came
together as fast as lightning, as slow as a glacier.
In a split second, Cara saw Breena's determined
scowl turn into a look of horror. She knew that
her own face was doing the same. Both riders
had realized that they had left their turn a
fraction too late.

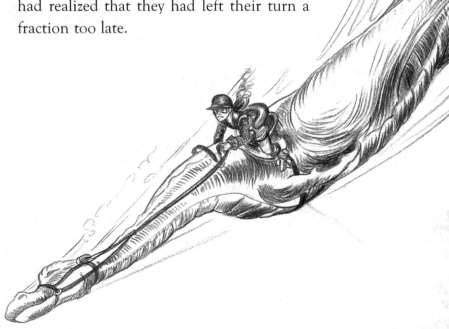

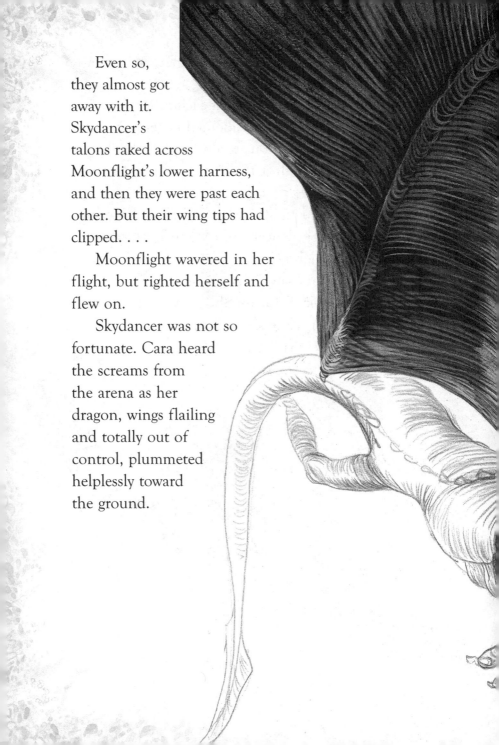

Even so,
they almost got
away with it.
Skydancer's
talons raked across
Moonflight's lower harness,
and then they were past each
other. But their wing tips had
clipped. . . .

Moonflight wavered in her
flight, but righted herself and
flew on.

Skydancer was not so
fortunate. Cara heard
the screams from
the arena as her
dragon, wings flailing
and totally out of
control, plummeted
helplessly toward
the ground.

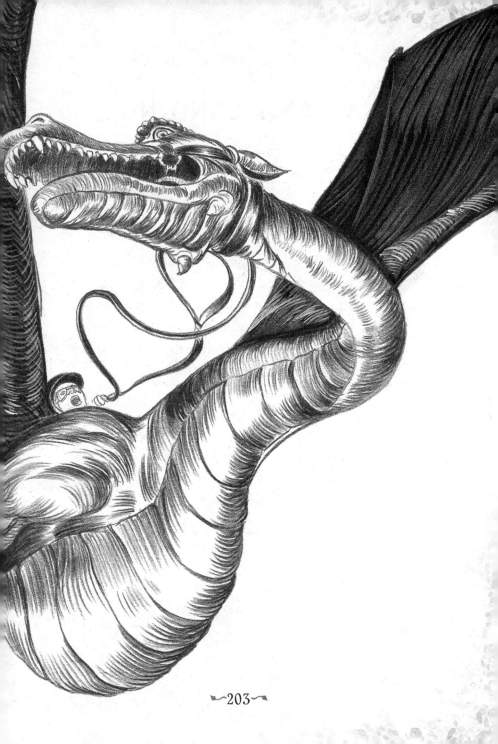

CRASH LANDING

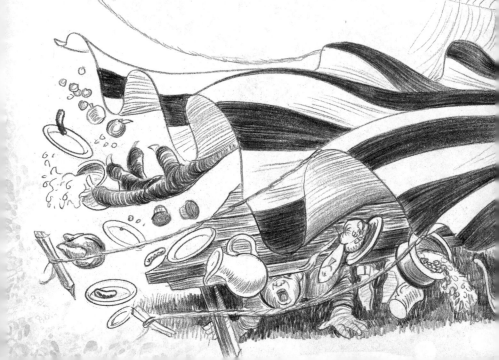

Skydancer's superb reflexes nearly saved them.

At the last second, the dragon managed to correct his spin and achieve stable flight. Cara pulled on the ear reins, urging Sky to pull up—not that the dragon needed any urging—but they were still in a dive and, by that time, just too low.

They shot over the arena, sending panic-stricken spectators in the highest tier of seats scrambling for cover, and careered across the meadow beyond, Sky's talons brushing the grass. For a moment, Cara hoped that they might be able to climb to safety. Then she saw a row of pavilions directly in their path, and shut her eyes.

The first they hit was the refreshment tent. Sky's wings ripped the canvas from its moorings, and his body slammed into the long trestle tables laden with

Gerda's choicest delicacies. Pies, cakes, and puddings exploded, sending gouts of meat and gravy, cream and custard flying left and right. Tarts and flans whizzed here and there like stones skimmed across a pond. Flagons of heather ale and jugs of wine and mead leapt into the air, emptying their contents in all directions. The members of Gerda's kitchen crew unlucky enough to be in the tent screamed and went down like ninepins.

Cara and Skydancer plowed on, leaving a trail of destruction in their wake. The few spectators who were not already in the arena hurled themselves out of harm's way. Dogs fled, howling. Lines of bunting snapped like spider silk and wrapped themselves around the dragon's hurtling body. One of Sky's wings demolished the first-aid tent (which, as Galen later acidly pointed out, at least gave the surgical team the chance to practice their skills on each other for once).

A chestnut stall went flying, sending its wares shooting about like sizzling hailstones. More tents collapsed, their guy ropes cut or pegs uprooted by Sky's wings or by the ever-increasing collection of debris he was carrying with him. But by now the dragon's headlong slide across the showground had slowed considerably, and when they hit a hoopla stall, Cara and her battered dragon jolted to a dead stop, in a cloud of dust and a chaotic jumble of broken timber, flailing ropes, and torn canvas.

Cara sat perfectly still for a moment, waiting for the feeling that the whole world had just reared up and hit her in the face to subside. As her senses returned to normal, she became aware of one terrible fact: Sky was not moving.

Though she was horribly shaken, there was now only one thought in Cara's head. "Sky!" she cried. She undid the buckles holding her in the saddle and slid to the ground. Wading through the remains of the stall, she reached Sky's head and threw her arms around his muzzle. "Sky! Are you hurt? Oh, Sky!"

She was beside herself with grief and terror. Tears stung her eyes and a wail of despair tore at her throat. Sky could be dead—and if he was, it was all her fault for getting into a stupid, pointless argument with Breena. Cara's heart hammered against her ribs, she felt cold and sick. . . .

Then the pile of debris covering Sky heaved and rippled. Cara almost fainted with relief. Skydancer shook himself like a dog and tried to stand, but found himself hampered by debris. He gave a snort of complaint.

"Sky! You're alive! It's all right! I'm here—I'll get you out, don't worry. . . ." Cara frantically began hauling at lengths of canvas and bunting, but her efforts came to little until stable hands and spectators began to show up with knives to cut away the wreckage.

Huw arrived at a run. He pulled his daughter away from Skydancer and spun her around to face him. "Cara! Are you all right?"

"Yes, Da, I'm fine, but Sky's trapped."

Huw took a deep breath. "All right." Cara realized that her father had been terrified on her behalf and was making a great effort to pull himself together. "First things first." He slipped a knife from the sheath at his belt and began to hack at a rope. Cara tugged on the rope to haul it clear of Sky's body in case the knife should slip. As the rope parted, another pair of hands seized the next one. Cara glanced up to find herself working alongside Drane, who looked pale but resolute.

As soon as the last of the ropes and canvas had been cut away, Sky surged to his feet and flexed his wings. He hissed and grimaced as his strained muscles protested, but he was able to extend both wings.

"No serious damage, it seems." Alberich Dragonleech had materialized beside Huw and was eyeing Skydancer with an air of professional appraisal. "Amazing. I'll carry out a detailed examination, of course. Your beasts must bear charmed lives, Dragonmaster."

Cara bit her lip. Her legs were trembling, her hands shaking. She rested her forehead against Skydancer's scaly brow and stroked his head while Sky crooned reassuringly. Alberich spotted Drane and called him over to assist as he began his examination.

"Cara!"

Breena, out of breath from running, pushed her way through the growing throng of onlookers. She stood, white-faced and irresolute, at the edge of the crowd.

Cara turned to face her. "He . . ." Her voice wasn't working. She swallowed hard and tried again. "He's all right, Breena, Sky's all right. We both are. Is Moonflight?"

Breena nodded and gave an inarticulate sob. She closed her eyes and wrapped her arms around herself, shivering as though from a sudden chill.

Huw had regained command of himself. "Breena," he said in a low voice, "take Moonflight back to her stable and make her comfortable. Alberich will come as soon as he is free. You will do no more flying today."

Breena stared, speechless, at the Dragonmaster as all her hopes and dreams came crashing to the ground. At the sight of her stricken face, Cara instantly forgot their quarrel. "Da, you can't! You can't stop Breena from flying in the Intermediate Clear if Moony's fit. It's her last chance to qualify. . . ."

"Cara." The Dragonmaster didn't raise his voice, but his tone was iron-hard. "You could have been killed today. Both of you. I hold you both responsible and equally to blame. You have both forfeited your right to represent Dragonsdale at this showing. I shall say no more at present. Cara, you will remain with Skydancer while Alberich examines him. Breena, you have your instructions."

Breena said, "Yes, Dragonmaster." As though in a trance, she turned meekly and made her way back through the crowd. Cara watched her go, stunned by this latest catastrophe. Poor Breena!

Huw gazed back at the trail of devastation left by Skydancer's crash landing. In the distance, Gerda was wringing her hands over her spoiled feast, while the surgical team tried to figure out how to operate with most of their stretcher-bearers on stretchers.

Mistress Hildebrand broke away from a hurried consultation with a gaggle of stable hands and marched over. "No serious injuries among the spectators or crew, Dragonmaster, thank goodness," she reported with customary brusqueness. "Luckily, most people were in the arena watching the display when Cara treated us to that exhibition of agricultural flying." She gave Cara a frosty look.

"Thank you, Hildebrand. Will you go back to the arena and get the competition under way?" Huw gestured at the wreckage. "I'm needed here. I've all this mess to clear up"—his gaze fell on a small knot consisting of the owners of the smashed stalls, who were muttering together angrily—"and compensation to pay, I expect. Ask Gerda to do what she can about the refreshments, but I think for once we may have to send our guests away hungry."

Mistress Hildebrand nodded and darted another disapproving frown at Cara. "They say accidents come in threes," she said. "I wonder who'll be next." She stalked off. Huw gave his daughter a parting glance and followed, shaking his head.

Alberich straightened up from his minute nose-to-tail examination of Skydancer and pinched his hooked nose between his fingers. "Hmmm." He turned to Drane. "Well? What do you think?"

"Me?" Drane gawped. Then he collected himself and said, "Uh . . . well . . . I think he has a muscle strain in his left wing—he's holding it awkwardly, like geese do when they're hurt. . . ."

"Yes—trauma to the flexor alae major. What else?"

"Um . . . some of the scales along his breast and his belly are missing or damaged, so he'll be pretty bruised underneath, I should think. He's sore right there . . ." Drane pointed to a spot behind the dragon's foreleg shoulder. ". . . so he may have cracked a rib, I've seen that happen to kine—but his breathing is all right, so it's probably just pulled muscles. I think that's it."

"I agree. Treatment?"

"Ah—well, on the farm we used to put poultices on cuts to clean out dirt. . . ." Drane shrugged helplessly. "I don't know whether that works on dragons."

"It does," Alberich told him. "See to it, will you? Poultices where scales are missing, cold compresses on the muscle strains and the worst of the bruising. Ice, too, if you can get it." He nodded. "Very good. Best get him back to his stable while I check on the other casualty." He strode away.

Drane stared after the departing dragonleech. "He asked me what I thought. He actually asked me what I thought!" His chin lifted a little.

In a small voice, Cara said, "Drane—will you help me with Sky? Please?"

Drane shook himself. "Oh—yes, of course—but I have to find Wony first. She wanted to come when she saw you crash, but I wouldn't let her. I thought you might be . . ." He flushed. "Well, you know . . . anyway, I told her she had to stay with Bumble. He was very upset—all the dragons were."

Cara became aware of the background chorus of hoots and roars from distressed dragons in the paddock. She groaned. "I'll have to try to calm them down—they can't fly a competition in that state." She squared her shoulders. "I'll walk Sky across to the paddock so they can see he's all right—that should help. I'll see you back at the stables, agreed?"

Drane nodded and hurried off. Cara turned to Sky. "What do you think, boy? Can you walk that far?"

Sky gave an affirmative honk. Cara set off toward the paddock and her dragon followed, stepping out proudly and only limping a little.

When Breena led Moonflight into the stable yard, the first person she saw was Hortense. She was standing right in front of the door to Moonflight's stable, so Breena could not ignore her.

"I saw what happened," she said in a voice that was soft and sympathetic, but belied by the gleam in her eyes. "Is Moonflight all right?"

"Yes," said Breena, who had no wish to discuss her dragon's injuries with Hortense. The High Lord's daughter stood aside as Breena led Moonflight into her stall, then followed them in.

"Poor Breena," she said. "That was your last chance to qualify for the Junior Championships, wasn't it?"

"Yes," said Breena.

"And I don't suppose you'll ever get into the guard flight now. It's so unfair. And it's all Cara's fault."

Breena said nothing.

And then Hortense made a big mistake.

She laid her hand on Breena's arm and said softly, "I just want you to know, if you ever need a friend . . ."

Breena stared at Hortense's hand with loathing. Then she shrugged it off and rounded on Hortense with an expression so ferocious that the High Lord's daughter gasped and took a step back.

Breena's voice was harsh, low, and vicious. "Understand this, Hortense. I've just nearly killed my best friend. I don't suppose she'll ever speak to me again, and small blame to her. I've wrecked my last chance of ever being Junior Champion or ever joining the guard flight. If you want the truth, I feel so low I could walk under a snake's belly without taking off my hat.

"But if you think I've sunk so low that I'd ever want you for a friend, you're very much mistaken. I'm a thousand times a fool for ever listening to you pouring your poison in my ears, when I know you for what you are—a mean, greedy, spiteful, treacherous imp of mischief who never had a kind thought in her head or a generous bone in her body."

Hortense stood openmouthed with shock and outrage at the sudden attack.

"Now," rasped Breena, "take your stupid, wicked apology for a face out of my sight before I spoil it for you!"

Hortense's mouth worked with fury for a moment. Then she hissed like an angry wyvern, spun on her heel, and ran from the stable.

Breena looked around, breathing deeply.

"Moony," she said, "are you up for a little flight?" Moonflight hooted and pawed at the cobbles, striking sparks with her talons. Breena felt along the front edge of her dragon's wing, where it had clipped Skydancer's. "Is your wing all right?"

Moonflight hooted again, as much as to say, "Me? Hurt? The very idea!"

"Come on, then. I know just where we can go to be alone."

Breena led her dragon into the yard and climbed into the saddle. From the distant arena she heard a roar of approval and the rain-on-roof noise of applause greeting a clear round. Breena closed her eyes. The stable, the showing, all her fears and ambitions seemed very remote and unreal.

She flicked the reins. With a beat of her mighty wings, Moonflight took to the air. Dragon and rider flew north, away from the arena. Dragonsdale became very small below them, growing indistinct in the haze, then becoming lost to view entirely.

That is how it came about that when Alberich Dragonleech arrived, he found he had no patient to check.

And that is also how it came about that Breena took Moonflight off without checking her harness, and without spotting the deep grooves that Skydancer's claws had made in the leather as he and Moonflight had come together over the arena.

Breena and Moonflight flew beyond Merfolk Bay and over the moorland between it and the Home Sound, the long inlet that led from the open sea to the island capital of South Landing. She and Moonflight crossed the sound and flew along the coast beyond. Before long, Breena found what she was seeking—a part of the cliff top shaped like a pard's head.

"This is the place, Moony," she called. "No one will find us here." She turned Moonflight's head toward a small cove hidden by cliffs on three sides, visible only from the sea.

As she did so, the damaged belly strap holding Moonflight's saddle in place parted with a sharp snap. The saddle shifted. Breena gasped, instantly running through her mind all she had been taught about emergency action in such a situation. She must undo the tether and her safety belt, and discard the saddle, riding bareback until Moonflight could land safely. . . .

She fumbled at the buckles. As she did so, the breast-strap failed. Just as Breena unclipped the last buckle, the saddle slipped from Moonflight's back.

Breena's feet slid from the stirrup irons. The reins were torn from her hands.

With a despairing cry, she fell away and plunged into the sea.

MISSING

"I know it hurts," said Cara. "But it has to be done." She held up a lantern to inspect Skydancer's bruised foreleg and began dabbing carefully at it with a dripping cloth. "Alberich said this will help to reduce the inflammation." Sky hooted his annoyance and shifted uncomfortably on his sleeping platform.

Following the accident, Cara had returned Skydancer to his stable to tend to his injuries, and had seen nothing of the day's competitions. A roar from the spectators had occasionally made her glance up, but after what had happened, all she was concerned with was Skydancer's well-being. Even when the crowds began to drift away, Cara had remained with Sky, racked by the memory of the accident and the knowledge of how much worse it could have been.

"Still here?" Drane's head appeared out of the dark, looking over the bottom stable door.

Cara gave him a wan smile. "Where else would I be?"

Drane shrugged and let himself into the stable. He took a cloth from the bucket of cold water at Cara's side and tended to another of Skydancer's bruises. The dragon gave him a martyred look but made no protest.

"Are you all right?" he asked.

"I've had better days."

"It's been a bad sort of a day all around," Drane agreed. "Wony's down in the dumps because Bumble didn't fly well—but then, the rest of our dragons did no better."

Cara groaned. "That's my fault. They were all upset by what happened to Sky. How did the rest of the showing go?"

"Well-l-l . . ." Drane considered for a moment. "Gerda's in shock, Mistress Hildebrand has resigned again, your father has spent all day apologizing to everyone he meets, and, just to make him feel better, Lord Torin has been going around telling everyone that it was the worst showing ever. Apart from that, it went very well."

Cara sighed and shook her head. "Poor Da," she said. "It's all my fault."

"And Breena's," said Drane, "and Hortense's."

Cara looked puzzled. "What's she got to do with it?"

"I did warn you." Drane squeezed out his cloth and dipped it back into the bucket. "I told you Hortense was always hanging around here. I'm sure as eggs is eggs she was up to no good. Even Gerda heard that she'd been stirring it up between you and Breena." He gave Cara a hard stare. "Why did you throw the competition at Clapperclaw?"

"Who says I threw—?"

"Oh, come on, Cara! Everybody knows. Why did you do it?"

Cara flushed. "Well, I overheard Hortense talking to one of her cronies, and she said a real friend would let Breena win. . . ."

Drane closed his eyes. "Do you really think Hortense cares whether anyone wins anything, apart from her and her precious friends? And isn't it a bit odd that they were talking about that just where you could hear it, when you'd only gone to the refreshment tent because of a message from Wony that she never sent?"

"Are you saying that I was supposed to overhear that conversation?"

"Well done," said Drane acidly. "I knew you'd get there in the end."

Cara closed her eyes. "The worst troublemaker in Seahaven, that's what Breena called Hortense. And I knew it as well as she did, and I still . . ." She let out a groan.

"Did Hortense speak to you today?" demanded Drane. "Before the display?"

Cara nodded. "She said Breena had told her I was pulling out of the Finnglassian Death Roll too early."

"Funny thing," said Drane. "I spotted her talking to Breena a few minutes before she came over to talk to you.

I wonder if she told Breena that you'd said the same thing about her."

"You saw her talking to Breena? And you didn't tell me?"

Drane pursed his lips. In merciless imitation of Cara's words by the Dragonsbeck, he said, "Maybe Breena likes having Hortense around. If they want to be friends, it's nothing to do with me."

Cara's eyes stung. A hard knot formed in her stomach and she felt sick. Had Hortense been turning her and Breena against each other all these months? She suddenly knew that Drane was right. An image of Hortense as a spider formed in Cara's mind: a black, foul creature, spinning a web of half-truths, lies, and deceit, drawing Cara and Breena in like a couple of flies, ready for her to gorge on . . .

"I've been an absolute fool," she said, "haven't I?"

"You won't get any arguments from me." Drane was silent for a moment. Then he dropped his cloth back into the bucket. "Your father said to tell you that he wants to see you and Breena."

"Poor Breena." Cara sighed. "All right. Will you tell her?"

Drane nodded and stood up. But before he reached the door, it was flung open and Wony burst in.

"Have you seen her?" she demanded. "Have you seen Breena?"

Cara and Drane exchanged glances. Cara said, "Isn't she with Moonflight?"

"She may be," said Wony distractedly. "I can't find Moony either."

"What are you talking about?" Cara suddenly felt cold.

"I can't find them anywhere. And I can't find anyone who's seen them since the Dragonmaster told Breena that she wasn't to take part in the Clear Flight."

Cara was aghast. "But that was hours ago. Where is she?"

Wony bit her lip and shook her head.

"Maybe she's just gone off somewhere to be by herself," said Drane.

"She wouldn't stay out after dark," said Cara. "Something's wrong." She stood up quickly. "I'm going to see my da."

The moon, more than three quarters full, hung in the sky, washing the small beach in a silver-blue light, illuminating the figures of a girl and a dragon lying next to each other on the hard, round pebbles. As the waves ebbed and flowed across the shingle, Moonflight nuzzled at Breena's limp body, making little crooning noises in an attempt to get a response from her mistress.

Breena half opened her eyes and flapped an arm at the dragon. "No, Moony. Get back to your stall." Then, slowly, memory worked its way through the fog of her mind.

She remembered the jarring shock as she'd hit the icy water, the muffled roaring and clicking in her ears as her waterlogged riding garments dragged her down beneath the waves. She remembered kicking for the surface again and again, feeling like her lungs were about to explode, and the cry of deliverance she had given as her head had finally burst from the sea's deadly embrace. She remembered the sting of saltwater spray lashing into her eyes, and Moonflight's desperate cries as she circled above. The white-hot stabbing pain in her shoulder as the dragon, finally overcoming her fear, swooped down to pluck her from the foaming water. The roar of the great rogue wave that came thundering into the cleft, a wall of water that had risen up and torn Moonflight from the sky, sending her and Breena tumbling into a seething maelstrom of grit, sand, and bubbles.

Her final memory was of being flung against the rocks, and the shocking, unendurable pain that shot through her right arm. After that, mercifully, she remembered no more.

Breena rolled over onto her side—and groaned. Every muscle and bone in her body ached, especially her right arm, which throbbed with pain when she tried to move it. Slowly she dragged herself to her feet and patted her anxious dragon. *We're alive!* she thought. *Both of us!* She wished she felt better about it.

She looked around the small beach and to the cave beyond.

With her one good arm, Breena lifted Moonflight's muzzle so that she could look into her eyes. "Moony, come on, there's a cave in the cliffs—we need to get to it. We'll get away from the water and sort ourselves out. Then we can fly out of here and get back home. Come on, girl, come on."

The dragon struggled to her feet and Breena gave a gasp of horror. Moonflight's left wing was hanging down by her side, limp and useless.

"Oh, no, Moony!" Breena knelt by her dragon's side, inspecting the sail. The membranes were torn and the large bone at the leading edge seemed to be broken. "Moony!" groaned Breena. "Oh, Moony!" Then she buried her face in Moonflight's flank and sobbed and sobbed.

When there were no more tears left for her to cry, Breena stood up and stroked Moonflight's neck. "Come on, Moony."

She turned to face the cave. In the moonlight, its mouth looked sinister and frightening, yet familiar. Breena had only caught a glimpse of it from the air—the overhanging cliffs hid it well—but she recognized it.

She and Moonflight had reached their destination after all—just six dragonlengths too low. Breena had intended to land on the cliff top.

But there was no doubting it. The rocky maw that lay before them was the Cave of Sighs.

Cara tapped at the door of the study and entered without waiting for a reply. Her father was talking to Galen.

He swung to face her, frowning at the interruption. "Cara—"

"Da," blurted Cara, "Breena's missing."

The Dragonmaster's brow furrowed. "What?"

"She's gone. So's Moonflight."

Huw leaned back on the edge of his desk. "You'd better tell me about it."

Cara explained the situation, the words tumbling over one another in her anxiety.

Galen was unimpressed. "She's probably sulking somewhere," he growled. "She's been like that for weeks now—disappearing for hours at a time." He shook his head. "Typical female hysterics! She'll turn up once her belly starts to rumble with hunger."

Huw gave him a cold look. "I am neither female nor hysterical, but I don't consider the failure of one of my riders to return before nightfall to be a trivial matter."

Galen held the Dragonmaster's gaze for a moment. Then he dropped his eyes.

"Very well," said Huw. "Send messengers to the other stables. She's likely found herself benighted and taken refuge with one of them."

Galen nodded and turned to go.

"But, Galen." Huw's voice was grim. "In case there is no news—have the guard flight ready to search at daybreak."

*   *   *

Dragonsdale was astir at first light. Galen led Nightrider from his stable and peered through the cold, persistent drizzle of rain at the gray clouds that crept sulkily across the sky. "A lousy morning for a search," he grunted. "And this fog has set in for the day, with worse to come tomorrow, I'll be bound."

A flapping of gigantic wings announced the arrival of the last messenger dragon. Huw spoke briefly to the messenger, then turned to Galen. "She's not been seen at Wyvernwood. That's all the stables accounted for, and no sightings."

"Then it's up to us." Galen turned to the riders of the guard flight. "Wet weather gear," he ordered. "Iron rations and waterproof flares for every rider. And if you can't see anything, or you or your dragon are too cold and tired to stay out, give up and come back here. I'd rather have a milksop who can fly again tomorrow than a hero who has to take to his bed."

The riders grinned ruefully.

"Mount up!" Galen commanded.

One by one, the guard flight took to the air.

Cara, dressed in flying gear and making for Skydancer's stable, was stopped by Huw's stern voice. "Where do you think you're going?"

"To help look for Breena. Da, it's my fault she's lost. . . ."

"Your dragon is unfit to fly," Huw told her in uncompromising tones.

"But, Da, she's my friend."

"It's a pity it took you so long to remember it. Do you intend to add to your dragon's injuries with yet more willfulness?" Cara hung her head. "Then do as you're told for once. You will not fly anywhere today."

The rest of the day was a torment for Cara. She tended Sky for a while, until Alberich came in to examine him and said pointedly that what he needed most of all was rest. She got under Gerda's feet until she was banished from the kitchen. She could not settle to anything. Long before sunset, she was in the stable yard with Wony, scanning the skies, waiting for the guard flight's return.

But when they flew in, travel-stained and weary, her worst fears were realized. The guard flight had searched the whole day, high and low—but of the missing girl and her dragon, there was no sign.

THE SEARCH

As they mounted up the next morning, the riders of the guard flight exchanged dour looks. Overnight, the weather had taken a turn for the worse: Visibility was lower, the rain heavier and more persistent. And the wind was picking up.

Cara waited until the official searchers, their flying leathers concealed beneath heavy oilskin capes, had taken off to resume their search. As soon as the yard was deserted, she led Skydancer from his stable. She moved briskly, anxious to get away before her father or Mistress Hildebrand could appear and forbid her to fly. So she jumped a mile when a voice said, "Going somewhere?"

"Drane!" Cara glared at him. "Don't creep up on me like that! What are you doing up so early, anyway?"

Drane gave her a jaundiced look. "Up early? I haven't been to bed!" He held up bruised and bleeding fingers for inspection. "Alberich Dragonleech collared me to help him with the dragons who came in exhausted from yesterday's search. I've spent all night drying out wet gear and rubbing liniment into sore muscles."

"Oh," said Cara guiltily. She had spent the night asleep—or, at least, trying to sleep.

"Are you supposed to be flying today?" Drane asked her. "Is Sky fit enough?"

"Don't you start! I checked him over while the guard flight were rattling about. He's still a bit sore, but he's fine."

"You shouldn't be going off on your own, though."

"I've got to do something! Don't say anything to my father."

Drane sighed. "I won't."

"Thanks." Cara put a hand on Drane's arm. "And thanks for helping."

Drane shrugged. "I can't fly a dragon," he said gruffly, "so I'm doing what I can." He stretched and gave a yawn. "I'm going to bed. Good night. Good morning. Whatever."

Cara watched him go for a moment, then climbed into the saddle and flicked the reins. Rider and dragon rose into the wet, sullen sky.

* * *

Breena stood on the pebbled beach with her arm around Moonflight's neck. She gazed at the retreating sea and considered their options.

They could wait to be rescued. Dragonsdale must have realized by now they were missing and mounted a search. But so far, they had seen no signs of anyone looking for them. This was not surprising. Nobody knew where they were. The Cave of Sighs was on one of the least frequented parts of the coast, and the beach where Breena stood was almost invisible from the air.

And if they were found, what then? The cliffs around them were high, and the cleft in the rocks that formed the bay was narrow and twisting. Even if rescuers did come, would they be able to get them out?

Climbing was out of the question—Breena could still hardly move her arm, and she was pretty sure Moonflight wouldn't be able to scale the cliffs without her wings for balance. Swimming was out, too. Breena couldn't swim, and Moonflight was now even more terrified of the sea than she had been before. In any case, even if they took to the water, there were no landing places along the coast for miles in either direction. They'd never make it.

There were other things to worry about. The lack of food and water, for one—Breena could slake her thirst from rainwater pools in the rocks, but these were too small for a dragon. Then there was Moony's condition. Breena was sure that the broken wing was not her only injury. Even from the few steps Moonflight was able to take in the narrow confines of the bay, it was clear that she was limping badly, and her breathing was labored. Breena had washed Moony's cuts with seawater and salved them with seaweed that she'd mashed up in a hollow in the rocks, as the fisherfolk did, but without splints there was nothing she could do about the wing.

However, the most pressing problem came not from injuries or lack of food but from the sea. The waves that washed into the little bay had subsided since their arrival, though Breena knew that as the wind gained in strength they would build again. But the greater and more implacable threat was the tide.

Being of fisherfolk stock, Breena understood the nature of tides. They came in and went out twice a day, but not always to the same level. At half moon, the difference between high tide and low tide was least; while at full moon and the dark of the moon, it was at its greatest. And tonight, the moon would be full.

This morning's high tide had driven Breena and Moonflight back into the Cave of Sighs. The water had reached Breena's waist. This afternoon's tide would be higher, the next tide higher still—until it reached its highest point, just after full moon tomorrow night. Breena watched the waves breaking. They were retreating now, but soon after the sun reached its zenith, they would begin to advance again.

Breena looked at the dark opening of the cave at her back. Every tide would drive them farther and farther into it. At the very least, she and Moony were in for a succession of soakings. But if the weather continued to get worse, building the tides still higher, Breena had a horrible idea that at the highest tide of all, the water might completely fill the cave. And if that happened . . .

She shuddered and tried to put the thought from her mind.

"I hope you like mussels," she told Moonflight, "because that seems to be about all there is to eat around here. Unless you prefer whelks?" Moonflight snorted and shook her head. "You're right," Breena told her, "whelks are disgusting."

That was when she saw the dragon.

It was only visible for a moment. The cleft allowed a view of a tiny patch of gray sky, and the dragon had disappeared from sight almost before she knew it was there. But Breena instantly cupped her hands around her mouth. "Hello!" she cried. "We're here! Down here!"

". . . ere, ere, ere . . ." echoed back from the surrounding rocks.

"Moony! They're looking for us!" Breena pointed. "Call them!"

For a moment, it seemed that Moonflight hadn't understood. But then Breena began to call again—"We're down here! By the cave!"—and Moonflight lifted her great head and bugled at the top of her lungs.

But it was to no avail. The dragon appeared once more, but this time it was higher and farther away, almost lost in the murk. Moonflight redoubled her efforts and Breena screamed her throat raw. But they did not see the searchers again. Eventually Moonflight fell silent. Her head drooped until her chin rested on the wet pebbles.

Breena sank to her knees and wept.

Cara returned from her search as the light faded. She felt drained. She had searched the high ground around Cloudhead, and every crag, slope, and gulley of the mountain itself, and had seen nothing but wheeling hawks and the occasional small herd of perytons. Galen and the guard flight were already back; the doors to their dragons' stalls were closed and she could hear voices from the house. Cara longed for the warmth of the kitchen and a big bowl of Gerda's piping-hot stew, but she untacked Sky and rubbed him down first, working with mechanical efficiency while her mind drifted.

She was jerked back to full consciousness when she left the stable just in time to see a small dragon fly unsteadily in over the stable block and make a clumsy landing in the yard. "Wony!" she called sharply. "What do you think you're doing?"

Wony dismounted stiffly. "I've been out with Bumble, to look for Breena."

"In this weather?" demanded Cara. "Are you mad? Bumble's still too young, and what if something had happened to you? Then we'd have had two lost dragons and riders to look for instead of one."

"Well, you weren't supposed to be out, either." Wony's lip quivered. "And I only wanted to help."

"I know, but . . ." Cara could see that further scolding was useless—and in any case, Wony was right. Cara had joined the search without permission, and her father would be furious. "Come on," she said, "let's get Bumble sorted out. I don't suppose you found any sign of Breena?"

Wony shook her head miserably. Cara took the small dragon's head harness and led him to his stable.

As she and Wony unthreaded straps and undid buckles, Cara said, "I'm beginning to think we've been looking for Breena in the wrong places. Galen thinks she was making for another stable, but why would she? And she wouldn't go hunting, not after what happened last time. So where would she go? Not Clonmoor, not Cloudhead, not the Walds, not South Landing, definitely not Clapperclaw Heights . . ." She shook her head. "Where would you go, Wony, if you were upset?"

"The sea," said Wony promptly. "I like the waves and the cry of the gulls."

"The sea." Cara thought back to her day with Breena at Spindrift Cove. Would Breena head for the sea? She didn't get along with her family and had turned her back on the fisherfolk, but the sea had been part of her childhood. "You could be right," she said slowly. "But which bit of the coast would she go to? Seahaven has an awful lot of it." She undid another buckle—and stopped dead. "If she did go to the sea," she said with mounting excitement, "maybe the merfolk have seen her! Ronan would know." Her voice was sharp and decisive. "I'll go and find him. First thing tomorrow."

The bulk of Moonflight's body almost filled the cave.

It was dark. The walls trembled with the impact of the seas thundering against the rocks outside. This tide was the highest yet. It had driven them up the beach and forced Breena and her dragon farther and farther into the Cave of Sighs.

Water washed into the cave, slopping and gurgling, reaching farther and farther up Moonflight's body, forcing Breena to climb higher and higher to stay above it. When a big wash came in, only their heads remained above water.

Another thunderous roar filled the air as a great wave lashed the rocks. Moonflight keened in terror. Breena was shivering uncontrollably, her teeth chattering, but she stroked her dragon's muzzle constantly, murmuring words of encouragement as the water, relentless and chill as death, clutched at them.

"They will come, Moony. They will. They'll find us. We'll be all right." Breena's mind flashed back to the day at Spindrift Cove when Cara had pulled her out of the sea. But this time there was no friend to rescue her. "Oh, Cara," she whispered, her voice cracking. "Where are you? I'm sorry. I'm sorry. Come soon. Please . . . come soon. . . ."

THE STORM GATHERS

The search teams set off again soon after sunrise the following morning. Flying conditions were difficult: The gray drizzle of the previous days had been replaced by scudding clouds and a blustery wind. In spite of this, every fit dragon and rider in Dragonsdale was now committed to the search for Breena.

All full-time members of the guard flight were now leading improvised wings. Having given Cara a tongue-lashing for going out without permission the previous day, Huw had reluctantly agreed that both she and Wony could join Mellan's wing, which was to search closest to Dragonsdale, covering the hills between Merfolk Bay and Home Sound. Galen and Tord were heading farther north, to Curlew Downs and Lakeland, and Huw was not convinced that Skydancer was up to such a grueling journey.

However, this arrangement suited Cara. As they approached Merfolk Bay, she swooped down to fly alongside Mellan and asked him to let her go to speak with Ronan.

Mellan looked worried. "Well, I don't know, Cara. Galen doesn't like riders going off on their own. . . ."

"It won't take long," cajoled Cara. "And I have to be alone—Ronan won't show himself to anyone else. I think he can be a big help. Please."

Mellan sighed. "I'll probably be in trouble with Galen—not that that's anything new. Oh, all right, then."

"Thanks, Mellan!" Cara banked Skydancer sharply away before Mellan could change his mind.

She alighted on the rocks at the sea's edge and showed Sky what she wanted him to do by slapping the water of a rock pool with her hand. Sky caught on quickly, and beat at the waves with three

strokes of his tail. After the third repetition of the call, Ronan appeared.

But when Cara had explained the situation to him, the merboy's response was not encouraging. "Your friend is not in Merfolk Bay," he said. "If she were, my people would know. Breena and her sky-dragon never came here. I am sorry."

"But still," persisted Cara, "they could have gone to another part of the coast, couldn't they? Somewhere merfolk don't go?"

"They could," conceded Ronan. "Dolphins and porpoises bring us news, but they are not always easy to understand. And there are many places where even they do not go."

"Then will you help me? Breena's my best friend, and it's my fault she's missing. Our guard flight has been all over the moors and the Walds and they can't find her."

"Cara, I have my flock to tend. . . ." Ronan caught Cara's expression and sighed. "All right, I will help you search. I suppose I can take my flock with me. The exercise might do them good." He looked up at the racing clouds. "But, Cara, we have little time. The weather is worsening. A storm is coming—tonight. I do not know how much longer you and Skydancer will be able to fly. I will have to take Mordannsair and my flock to deeper water to escape the surge of the waves. And tonight, also, the tide will be at its height. If your friend is trapped at the sea's edge—even if she has survived so far—if we do not find her by sunset I am afraid it may be too late."

Breena stood on the beach and stared up at the cliff.

She was soaked through the skin. Her sodden clothes clung to her. She was shivering and her teeth were chattering. She could not remember a time when she had been dry and warm.

The morning's tide had been the highest yet. She and Moonflight had barely survived it. The sea had flooded in to the extent that only a small pocket of air remained at the very back of the cave, and by the time the water receded, the air in this pocket had become so foul that Breena had almost fainted from breathing it.

She felt sick and weak. She could barely raise her right arm to shoulder height. But Breena was sure that she and Moony would not survive another high tide—and tonight's would be the highest of all. They had not seen another dragon since their second morning at the Cave of Sighs. They could not count on rescue. There was no alternative but to climb out of the bay.

"Come on, Moony. Follow me." Breena stepped onto a rock at the base of the cliff and reached for a handhold. The response from her injured arm made her gasp in agony, but she gritted her teeth and hung on until the first wave of pain had receded. Then, with aching slowness, she continued.

Watching as her mistress gained height, Moonflight crooned with anxiety. The higher Breena went, the louder and more frantic became her cries of distress at being left behind. At length, the dragon could stand it no more; she reared up on her hind legs, dug her talons into the rock, and began to climb.

Their progress was agonizingly slow. Even for an expert climber, the going would have been difficult, but for an injured girl and dragon, it was torture. Parts of the rock were hard and sharp, and Breena's hands were soon torn and bleeding from gripping the jagged stone. In other places, apparently solid rock crumbled beneath her fingers.

After much excruciating effort, she reached the halfway point of her climb. Her ears were full of the screams of gulls, skimming effortlessly along the cliff face up which she was hauling herself with such difficulty. The sea pounded relentlessly at the rocky shore three dragonlengths below. Finding a secure hold, she paused, looked up—and gave a moan of dismay.

The cliff above her was much worse than anything she had tackled so far. It was steeper and smoother, with fewer hand- and footholds—and just at its edge, high above, there was an overhang.

Breena steeled herself. Whatever the difficulties, she must carry on. She must guide Moonflight out of the refuge that had become a death trap.

She looked down at Moonflight, clinging to the cliff a dragonlength below. "Come on, Moony," she cried. "You can do it!"

But as Breena called to her, Moonflight lost her grip. Her talons tore at the rock, seeking a new hold. She flapped in desperation, trying to take some of her weight with her wings, but the broken one flailed uselessly.

Moonflight fell. An avalanche of dislodged stones followed her as she tumbled helplessly down the cliff face and crashed onto the pebbles of the beach. She twitched once, then lay still.

"Moony!" Breena's cry echoed around the cliffs. She immediately started down, almost falling as she lost a foothold. She clung to the rock, trembling. She wanted to get down to Moonflight, she must hurry, hurry, but she knew it would do her dragon no good if she fell. She forced herself to be calm, and set off once more, picking out her holds with care, going slowly, deliberately, feeling that time had stopped.

After what seemed an eternity, she reached the beach and staggered over to where Moony lay. Breena cradled her dragon's great head in her arms, forgetting her own aches and pains in her distress. "Moony—are you all right? Please, Moony . . ."

Moonflight forced open an eye and gave a feeble hoot. Breena let out her breath in a gasp of relief. She fought to bring her breathing under control and stop trembling.

"Come on, Moony," she said in as businesslike a voice as she could muster, "let's see what the damage is. Up you get."

Moonflight hooted a protest, but struggled groggily to her feet. Breena examined her carefully, fearful of what additional injuries she might find. But dragons were built to withstand bad landings, and the fall had not been so great. Her injuries seemed no worse than they had been before.

Nevertheless, it was clear that Moony would never be able to scale the cliff. Where did that leave the two of them?

Breena had made the climb halfway, and could probably manage the rest. But as she looked up at the cliff again and remembered the effort her attempt had cost, her heart failed her.

They could climb above the cave and wait for the high tide to recede—if they could cling on to the bare rock, lashed by wind, waves, and rain, for four hours or more. She didn't think she could do this, and she was absolutely certain that Moony couldn't.

If she tried to climb to the top again and fell, Moonflight would be alone. Even if she made it, what could she do? Go for help? But the nearest farms and villages were far inland, on the Walds, at least two days away on foot, and South Landing was even farther. The hills in between were infested with firedogs and howlers, maybe even pards. . . .

And there was no time. High above, the clouds parted, and the afternoon light cast shadows on the cliff. The sun was sinking; slowly, inexorably, night was drawing on. Night—and the highest tide of all.

"It's no use, Moony," Breena said softly. She knew in her heart that she and Moonflight would not survive another night in the cave, and she had given up all hope of rescue.

"Never mind, Moony," she said. "If this is to make an end of us, at least we'll be together."

Mellan called off the search when Wony urgently signaled that she needed to land. He brought his wing down near a lonely barn used as a winter shelter for grazing kine.

Wony almost fell off Bumble, and Cara immediately rushed to support her.

"I'm sorry, Cara." Wony was distraught. "It's Bumble — he's worn out. He needs a rest."

"You look as if you could do with one yourself." At a nod from Mellan, Cara led her young friend and her dragon to the barn and made them comfortable in the new-mown hay. "Don't sneeze," she told Bumble sternly. "One trickle of flame from you and the whole place will go up."

Bumble blinked at her as if to say, "Who? Me?" and tucked his nose under his wing.

Cara returned in time to hear Mellan say, "We're agreed, then. We've covered our search area and found nothing. We're all tired, cold, wet, and hungry, and the weather's getting worse by the minute. There's no point in staying out any longer." There were nods from the weary searchers.

"Mellan," said Cara, "I have to check with Ronan. He may have found something."

Mellan sighed. "Well, I suppose we can give you a few minutes."

Cara was aware that some of the riders were looking less than delighted by this delay. "No, it's all right. You go back to Dragonsdale. I'll go to Ronan, then come back here and collect Wony, and we'll fly back together."

Mellan scratched his head. "Well, I suppose there's no point in us all hanging around. . . ." This was greeted with eager nods. "Galen really isn't going to like this." Mellan sighed again. "All right—move out!"

As the dragons took off with a mighty flapping of wings that sent showers of rainwater cascading in all directions, Cara led Skydancer back to the barn. She found Wony in tears. "Cara, I'm so sorry, Bumble just couldn't go on, I didn't mean to stop the search. . . ."

"It's not your fault," Cara told her gently. "Mellan was about to call off the search, anyway. It'll be dark soon, so we couldn't have gone on much longer. Come on, try and get some sleep while I go to see Ronan. Even if it's only a few minutes, you'll feel better."

Wony sniffed. "I don't feel sleepy."

"Just lie down," Cara told her. "Try to relax." Wony curled up with her head pillowed on her arm.

As she gazed down at her friend, Cara was visited by an extraordinarily vivid memory of a night in the kitchen at Dragonsdale House, soon after her mother had died. Cara had been weeping in her bedroom, and Gerda had brought her down and fed her a bowl of warming soup. Then Cara had rested her head in Gerda's lap. Shadows flickered across the pots and pans and the hanging bundles of herbs as the fire in the hearth burned fiercely. Two wyverns, Tricksy and Rainbow—ancestors of the wyverns that still lived in the kitchen to this day—lay curled up in front of the comforting flames.

"The fire burns," Gerda had said, stroking the knots from Cara's hair, "and the world turns, and tomorrow is another day."

Remembering, Cara stroked Wony's golden curls, and began to sing softly.

"Loolay, lullaby,
My sweet one, don't cry.
Lay down, my little one,
Let worry all begone.
For when dark falls the night,
All the dragons take flight,
To chase the darkness away,
Yes, to chase the darkness away.

Don't cry, don't sigh,
Sing a dragon lullaby,
And chase the darkness away.
And chase the darkness away."

Bumble, watching from his bed of hay, gave a chirrup and yawned. Wony's eyelids began to droop.

> *"Loolay, lullaby,*
> *Dragons will fly,*
> *As you lay down to rest,*
> *In the Isles of the Blest.*
> *And while you're a-sleeping,*
> *A pledge they're a-keeping,*
> *To chase the darkness away,*
> *Yes, to chase the darkness away.*
>
> *Don't cry, don't sigh,*
> *Sing a dragon lullaby,*
> *And chase the darkness away.*
> *And chase the darkness away."*

Wony's eyes closed. Cara withdrew her hand and sang:

> "*Don't cry, don't sigh,*
> *Don't cry, don't . . . sigh!*"

Sudden inspiration struck Cara. With a gasp, she sat bolt upright. "That's it!"

Wony blinked sleepily at her. "What's it?"

"That's what I've been trying to remember. What Breena told me, when we went to Spindrift Cove, about a place she knew. 'I know of a place where the sea weeps,' that's what she said. She called it the Cave of Sighs. Don't you see?" Cara leapt to her feet, positively dancing with excitement. "That's exactly the sort of place she'd go when she felt unhappy. That's where she is, I know it!"

Wony was suddenly wide awake. "Well, let's go and find her!"

"Yes, but . . ." Cara clenched her fists in frustration. "I don't know where the Cave of Sighs is!"

"No," said Wony slowly, "but Ronan would know, wouldn't he?"

Cara stared at her, openmouthed. "Wony, that's brilliant! Of course he would!"

"Well, what are we waiting for?" Wony scrambled to her feet.

"Just a minute," said Cara quickly. "You and Bumble are staying here."

"We are not!" Wony shot back. "Hunters fly in threes. Remember? That's what Galen told Breena. You, me, and Ronan makes three. I'm coming."

"But what about Bumble?"

Wony hugged her dragon. "Bumble's fine. He just needed a bit of a rest, didn't you, boy?" Bumble, who was indeed looking much more alert, warbled in agreement.

Cara reached a quick decision. "All right! Come on, then."

Outside, night was falling. The sun was setting below the western hills, turning the sky purple and the racing clouds vivid orange and bloodred. The wind howled around the barn and tried to tear the doors from their fingers as Cara and Wony fought to get Bumble out.

Seconds later, two dragons and their riders threw themselves into the wild sky and battled their way northeastward, riding on the wings of the storm.

RIDING TO
THE RESCUE

The last red traces of sunset were fading from the sky as they flew, and the fatal moon rose from the sea. Angry squalls marched across the horizon, black and threatening. Rank upon rank of cloud was massing to the east, spreading toward Seahaven like an invading army as Cara and Wony brought their dragons in to land on the shores of Merfolk Bay.

Cara stood on a rock and stared out over waves that were white-flecked with foam and spray as Sky lashed the water with his tail. Within a few seconds, Ronan appeared, swimming well clear of the dangerous swell. "Cara," he called, his voice almost lost in the howl of the wind and the roar of the sea, "I have searched all day and found no sign of your friend. . . ."

"But I think I know where she is!" cried Cara. "She's at the Cave of Sighs. Do you know it?"

Ronan was appalled. "Yes—it is to the north of Home Sound." He quickly described the location, adding, "But it is a terrible place, the haunt of sea lions and leopard seals. Merfolk never go there."

"We have to go there! That's where Breena is."

"Are you sure?"

For a moment, Cara hesitated. She wasn't sure, couldn't be sure—but if she faltered now, Breena could be lost. In a steady voice, she called, "I'm sure."

Ronan glanced at the sea and the sky. "The storm is upon us. I should help my brothers move our flocks to deeper water. . . ."

"Please, Ronan!"

Ronan shook his head in resignation. "Very well. But it is far away. And the water is rising. At high tide it will fill the cave, and if your friend is trapped . . ."

"Can you get us there in time?"

"Mordannsair can. Wait here." Ronan dived beneath the waves.

Wony stared, openmouthed, at the fading ripple where the merboy had disappeared. "That was . . . wasn't he . . . ? I've never . . . how did he . . . ?"

Cara wasn't listening. *I must tell Galen,* she thought. *But I have to go with Ronan—right now. I can't go back to Dragonsdale, there's no time. If I do, high tide will have come and gone by the time I get to the Cave of Sighs. Can I send Wony? But it's getting dark, and Bumble's tired, and the weather—can Wony fly back on her own? It's a lot to ask of her . . . but if it's Breena's only hope . . .*

Cara made up her
mind. "Wony," she said
firmly, "take Bumble and go back
to Dragonsdale. Tell Galen where
we're going."

Wony's face was a picture of dismay. "But I want to
come with you!"

"It's a long way," Cara told her, "and we have to get
there quickly—Bumble won't be able to keep up. Anyway,
I'll probably need help to rescue Breena." *If she's still there
to be rescued,* a treacherous little voice at the back of her
mind added. "The best way you can help her and Moony
is to fetch the guard flight. You heard what Galen told
Breena about what to do when a rider's in trouble—'One
to stay, one to go for help.'"

Biting back tears, Wony nodded. "All right."

Cara took her by the shoulders. "Can you remember
what Ronan said? About how to get there?" Wony
repeated Ronan's directions, and Cara gave her a parting
hug. "Off you go, then. Fly well."

Wony returned the hug, then turned and scrambled over the rocks to where Bumble was waiting. She didn't look back. Seconds later, the small dragon and its rider took off, and were instantly whipped away by the storm and lost to view.

A strange, bubbling scream echoed across the crashing waves. Cara peered out to sea, squinting against the wind and spray. Ronan's beautiful sea-dragon, Mordannsair, was rearing out of the water. As Cara stared, the creature called again, and Ronan, clinging to its back, beckoned and pointed northward.

Cara threw herself into Skydancer's saddle, and together they hurled themselves into the air, defying the storm.

It was a wild ride. Cara braced herself in the saddle and hung on. Above her, the moon rose higher into the tearing clouds. Below, Ronan and Mordannsair were dark shadows, speeding beneath the waves. Every thirty dragonlengths or so, the sea-dragon and its rider leapt from the sea in a graceful arc, seemed to hang suspended for a moment, then dived beneath the foaming water in a fountain of spray.

Cara and Skydancer were buffeted by the wind, flung about in the sky like autumn leaves. Squalls of driving rain tore at them, reducing visibility to less than a dragonlength. Several times Cara thought she had lost sight of Ronan—but always the white splash of the sea-dragon's dive, glinting in the moonlight, led her back to their course.

The race against storm and tide seemed to go on forever, but at last, weary, bruised, and half numb with the effort of clinging on, Cara spotted the dark loom of land to her left, and Ronan and Mordannsair turned toward the shore.

As Cara followed, an eerie wailing sounded in the night, clearly audible even over the howl of the storm. She knew it must be the voice of the Cave of Sighs. It rose and fell, crying a lament, mourning all the souls ever lost to the power of the storm.

The sea wept.

Breena clung, shivering, to Moonflight's neck while the cold water rose around them.

Even here in the cave, she could feel the power of the storm. During the previous tides the water had risen calmly and inexorably, lapping at the cave walls, but tonight Breena could hear the waves thundering outside her refuge, sending surges into the tiny space in which she and her dragon huddled. One moment, the water would reach Breena's chin. The next, it would fall to her waist—but the respite was only momentary. When the tide reached its full height, the water would engulf them altogether.

The wailing began so faintly that she could not be sure she had heard it. But with every passing minute, the sound grew in strength. A cold hand of fear clutched at

Breena's heart as all the childhood terrors of wraiths and witches, goblins and bogeymen rushed into her mind. Moonflight warbled anxiously.

But as the sound went on and nothing ghostly came gibbering out of the dark to get them, Breena gave a shamefaced chuckle. "What a pair we are, hey, Moony?" She patted her dragon's neck. "Here we are scared of a noise, when it's the water that's going to do us in. Maybe it's a ghost or a banshee come to wail at our ending. Morbid creature, I hope it drowns."

Breena had no way of knowing the actual cause of the sound: a long fissure in the rock, far too narrow to climb. It led from the back of the cave to the cliff top, so that when the water rose in the cave, a column of air blew through the natural organ pipe to produce the wailing. All Breena knew was that the water had not much farther to rise before she and Moonflight would be overwhelmed. Nothing could save them now. She felt strangely calm at the prospect.

As the wailing filled the cave, she felt for Moonflight's head and stroked her muzzle. "I can't see you," she told her, "but I'd be a lot more scared if you weren't with me." She sighed. "I've not been a good mistress to you, have I? I let you get hurt, and at the last I've brought you to this dreadful place. I didn't mean to. I'm sorry. Please forgive me." Breena kissed Moonflight on the forehead. "Good-bye, Moony," she said softly.

Dark shapes appeared in the water around the sea-dragon, swimming beside and behind it. For a moment, Cara thought they were just the shadows of the racing clouds; then she realized that the shapes were not moving together, but independently. They dashed forward and hung back, turn by turn. Three and four at a time, they came darting in to harry Mordannsair, snapping at his fins like a pride of pards stalking boar or kine. Though she could see neither mane nor spotted hide, Cara knew instantly what they were: sea lions and leopard seals. They were on the hunt, and Ronan's mount was their quarry.

Mordannsair's leaps grew more frequent, but the hunters matched the sea-dragon leap for leap, and every

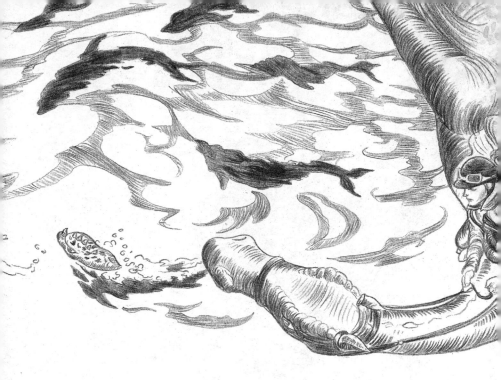

time Mordannsair dipped below the surface, they closed in. Cara's heart was in her mouth. She had not imagined that there would be so many of the beasts, or that they would be so ferocious. And she had persuaded Ronan to come here—he was in danger because of her! But as the wails of the Cave of Sighs echoed in her ears, Cara's fear gave way to rage. Ronan had led her here to rescue Breena, and these wretched, bloodthirsty beasts were not going to stop them now. She tightened her knees and pulled back on the leg reins. "Come on, Sky. Get them!"

Skydancer needed no further urging. He swooped down on the attackers, timing his dive to meet their leap. A roaring, seething jet of flame erupted into the middle

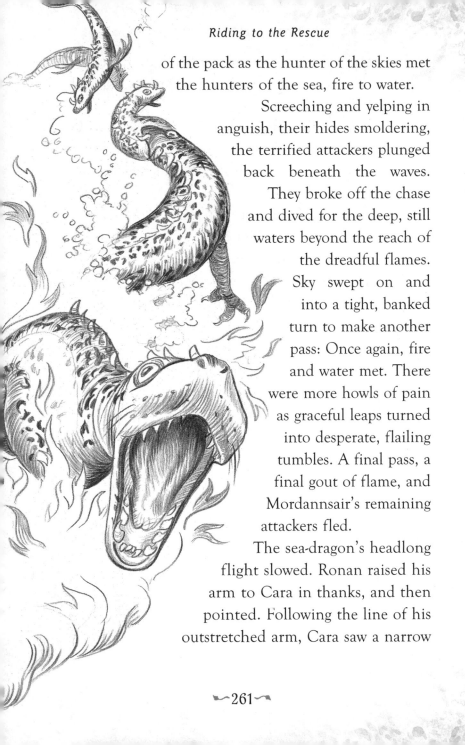

of the pack as the hunter of the skies met the hunters of the sea, fire to water.

Screeching and yelping in anguish, their hides smoldering, the terrified attackers plunged back beneath the waves. They broke off the chase and dived for the deep, still waters beyond the reach of the dreadful flames. Sky swept on and into a tight, banked turn to make another pass: Once again, fire and water met. There were more howls of pain as graceful leaps turned into desperate, flailing tumbles. A final pass, a final gout of flame, and Mordannsair's remaining attackers fled.

The sea-dragon's headlong flight slowed. Ronan raised his arm to Cara in thanks, and then pointed. Following the line of his outstretched arm, Cara saw a narrow cleft appear in the cliffs before her—and, on the cliff top, a rock in the shape of a pard's head, just as Ronan had described.

Cara turned Skydancer, and they flew back and forth along the cliff top. The white boulders and wiry plants gleamed dimly in the moonlight, but there was no sign of life.

Skydancer dived down to circle above Mordannsair. "They're not up there!" Cara called.

"They may be in the cave. Wait."

Mordannsair dipped underwater. A few moments later, the sea-dragon reappeared, closer inshore and alone.

Time passed. It could have been only a few seconds, but to Cara, struggling to keep Skydancer circling in the ferocious updraft of the storm wind battering the cliffs, it felt like an eternity.

Ronan reappeared. He waved, and shouted something that was blown away by the storm. Cara shook her head. Ronan nodded vigorously and beckoned.

Cara's heart leapt. The gesture could only mean one thing. He had found Breena and Moonflight! They must still be alive. . . .

Cara hesitated no longer. She came in to hover just above Ronan, with the thundering waves clutching at Sky's

talons. Then she tore off her heavy
flying jacket and kicked off her
boots. She unclipped her tether
and safety belt. She took a
deep breath, swung her
right leg over Skydancer's
neck—and dropped
into the sea.

THE CAVE
OF SIGHS

The water was cold. Waves battered Cara's head; spray lashed at her face. There was no time to take a breath. Salt water poured into her mouth. Cara began to drown.

And then Ronan was there, turning her face away from the waves, supporting her. "Cara—what are you doing? This is not safe for you!"

"I know that! But I can't do anything for Breena—" She broke off and spluttered as she swallowed more water, then continued, "up there in the sky. Is she in the cave? And Moony? Are they all right?"

"For the moment, yes, but the tide . . ."

"Can you get them out?"

"I do not know. I swam into the cave and met your friend. She thought I was a ghost."

"What? Why?"

"I do not know. I asked her to swim out with me but she said she wouldn't leave her sky-dragon. . . ."

"Take me to her."

"Come, then." Ronan put his arms around Cara's shoulders. With powerful strokes of his fish tail, he towed her toward the cliff. Two dragonlengths from it, he stopped. "We must swim underwater from here, or the swell will dash us against the rocks," he said. "It is a long way for you, I think."

"I can do it," said Cara bravely. Then she added, in a smaller voice, "As long as you're with me."

"Breathe deeply." Ronan waited while Cara took several gulping breaths, then said, "Now!"

They dived beneath the surface. Even here, Cara could feel the power of the waves as Ronan pulled her through the water. Everything was a dark blur; her ears were full of roaring; her body felt the tug of powerful currents and the brush of unseen weed. Her lungs tightened and her ears sang as Ronan swam deeper to avoid the wash of the waves on the cliff. The pressure eased as they entered the darkness of the cave, but by now Cara was desperate for air, every muscle in her chest bowstring-taut as she fought her need to breathe. . . .

And then her head broke water and she gulped down lungfuls of life-giving air, none the worse because it smelled strongly of dragon.

"Cara?" It was pitch-black inside the cave but Breena's voice was unmistakable. Cara reached out and found her friend. They hugged, rising and falling on the invading tide. Moony gave an anxious warble and both girls reached out to stroke and quiet her.

Breena had to raise her voice against the constant wailing from the fissure above her head. "Cara, you shouldn't be here."

Cara snorted. "That's a fine thing to say!"

"I mean it. You can't get us out, it's too late. The water will be over our heads in a moment. I'm sorry, Cara, it's all my fault. . . ."

"Shut up!" Cara felt like crying, but she knew she had to be firm and decisive. "There's no time for that now. There has to be a way to get you away from here. Ronan's here to help. Can you climb? Can Moony?"

"I can—just. But Moony has a broken wing. We tried to get up the cliffs, but she couldn't . . ."

"All right," said Cara. "Come on, we have to get you out."

Breena stiffened. "I'm not leaving without Moony."

"But there's no point in you both—"

"I mean it, Cara." Breena's voice was cracked and her teeth were chattering, but her determination was obvious. "I got Moony into this, and I'm not getting out unless she does. And that's final."

Cara fought down an urge to scream. She couldn't save them both, she just couldn't—Moony was terrified of the sea, she would never survive the storm. And with a broken wing she'd never be able to climb the cliff, unless . . .

. . . unless, somehow, she had another pair of wings.

"I've got a plan," said Cara. "Ronan? Can you take me back to Sky?"

"Yes."

"I'll be back soon," Cara told Breena. Without waiting for a reply, she dived back into the water.

The journey back to the open sea was bad, but not as bad as going into the cave had been, because this time Cara knew she could make it. Immediately she surfaced, she kicked her body as high out of the water as she could and waved to Sky. The dragon spotted her instantly and swept down. At a signal from Cara, he landed on the surface of the water, backing his wings and touching down hind legs first, like a swan, before coming to rest with his wings fluttering and his legs pumping in a gigantic doggy paddle.

Ronan stared. "I did not know sky-dragons could swim. I thought they were afraid of the sea."

"Sky isn't." With Ronan's help, Cara swam awkwardly to the dragon's side. "Sky, I need your saddle." She began to unbuckle the straps. Her fingers were clumsy from the cold, but eventually the saddle and harness came free. Cara pressed them into Ronan's arms. "Take these into the cave."

"And you?"

"I'll hang on to the reins—you can tow me along behind."

This worked, except that Cara tried to surface too soon inside the cave and banged her head on the rock ceiling. She had a moment of panic before Ronan returned to lead her to the diminishing air pocket where Breena and Moony were waiting.

Cara found the saddle and began to work on the reins, inwardly blessing Mistress Hildebrand for insisting that all her riders should be able to tack and untack a dragon blindfolded. She'd thought it a ridiculous waste of time—how often would a rider have to take off or put on her dragon's saddle and harness in complete darkness? Well, maybe only once . . . but if that once meant the difference between life and death . . .

"I'm shortening the reins," she told Breena, "and doubling them, for strength, and leading them around the saddle to make a sort of sling. Moony's wings aren't working, but Sky's are. He's not strong enough to lift Moony, but he can help her get up the cliff." She pulled at the straps. "Done! Now, help me to get the saddle on Moony."

In the dark and the ever-rising water, this was a slow and difficult task, but Cara and Breena had tacked dragons together many times before, and worked with an instinct born of long practice. Several times Cara had to dive down into the dark water to pass a breast- or belly strap around Moonflight's body.

By the time they had finished, the air pocket was reduced to little more than a bubble, and the water washed over their heads between breaths.

"That's it," Cara gasped. "Now, you go with Ronan and I'll lead Moony. . . ."

"Moony goes first," insisted Breena.

"We haven't time to argue! Moony won't go first; she won't go at all while you're still here. You know that."

"All right! But when we get out, you tell Sky to rescue Moony first. I won't be carried off and leave her in the sea."

"Yes. I promise. Trust me." In moments, the last of the air would be gone. Cara gave Breena a push. "Just get going!"

"Come," said Ronan. "Take three deep breaths. One — two — three — now!"

Cara heard Breena gasp. There was a swirl of water, and Moony set up an anguished keening that mingled with the wails of the cave. Cara took the dragon's head between her hands. "That's right—Breena's gone. And we have to go, too—right now. Come on, Moony—follow Breena!" She took a deep breath and tugged at the head harness. With a last hoot of loss and misery, Moonflight surged behind her, into the cold, inky-black water.

This time, the journey from the cave seemed to go on forever. Cara was tired, and Moonflight moved so slowly—she barely fit into the cave, and the water pushed her up against the ceiling. Cara had to keep pulling at the harness, urging the dragon to swim more deeply to avoid snagging her wings on the rocks. But at last a glimmer of moonlight above them showed that they were clear of the cave. Her lungs bursting, Cara kicked for the surface. Moonflight appeared beside her, struggling frantically against the rough water, bugling with terror. Sky spotted them and swept down.

There was no time to lose. At any moment, a wave could pick them up and hurl them onto the jagged rocks. Cara struggled onto Moonflight's back. Precariously balanced on the saddle and holding the reins as tightly as she could, she beckoned to Skydancer to hover closer.

"Take them, Sky!" She thrust out the reins, pointing at the cliff and making climbing motions with her hands. "Help Moony climb. Do you understand, Sky? Take the reins! Help Moony!"

Sky hovered indecisively. For a moment, Cara was in despair. Sky was the cleverest dragon she'd ever known.

He had to understand what she wanted him to do—he had to!

Then, to Cara's intense relief, Sky swept forward and snatched the reins from her hands. "Yes!" Cara pointed to the cliff top. "Lift, Sky! Up there! Take Moony up!"

She had done all she could. Cara threw herself into the water and fought her way through the waves until she was a safe distance from the rocks. She turned just in time to see Sky wait until a wave lifted Moonflight and flung her toward the cliff. As the wave broke beneath her, Sky flapped his wings in a frantic effort—and instead of being battered against the cliff by the wave, Moonflight landed, legs first, against it. Her talons scrabbled at the rock, tore free, scrabbled again—and gripped tight.

For a moment the two dragons held their positions. Then, feeling Sky's powerful wings pulling her upward, Moonflight started to climb away from the deadly waters.

"Cara! Here!"

Cara swam toward the sound of Ronan's voice. Eventually she saw him. It was all the merboy could do to keep Breena's mouth and nostrils clear of the water. Breena's head lolled against his shoulder; her eyes were closed.

"Breena!" Cara swam to Breena's side and tried to help Ronan support her. "We have to get her out of the water as soon as we can."

"Only your sky-dragon can do that."

"I know, and he can't leave Moony." Cara looked up at the cliff again. "Come on, Moony. Climb faster." She gave a groan. "Sky can't keep on hovering like that forever, and Breena needs him, too!"

But Cara's wish was not granted. The higher Moonflight climbed, the slower her progress became. She was tiring, and so was Sky. The less lift he could provide, the longer Moony was taking to rise from one claw-hold to the next. At length, just below the top of the cliff, she stopped altogether. Skydancer was clearly in trouble; his head drooped and his wing beats were labored.

"Oh, no!" Cara's voice was despairing. "They're nearly there, they can't fail now—go on, Sky, go on, Moony, go on!"

Sky made a desperate effort to lift Moonflight. The dragon reached up—and slipped back. She dug her talons into the rock to stop herself from sliding, but she could do no more. The overhang had defeated them.

And then, even above the roar of the storm and the wailing from the Cave of Sighs, Cara heard another sound—the bugling of many dragon voices and a rush of dragon wings. Half a dozen dragonriders brought their beasts sweeping in from the sea to land on the cliff top. Cara recognized the silhouette of Nightrider, Galen's great Ridgeback Charger. Wony had made it back to Dragonsdale and the guard flight had come!

Cara was too far away to hear orders, and the wind was against her. She could only watch as some of the riders let themselves down the face of the cliff on ropes, carrying coils of heavier rope, which they hastily lashed to the improvised sling supporting Moonflight. The ropes tightened. Cara knew that, on the cliff top and out of sight, the dragons of the guard flight must be straining at the ropes like oxen pulling a plow through hard ground.

Moonflight rose bodily up the cliff. She paused for a moment, suspended over the edge, then disappeared from view as the rescuers hauled her to safety.

Cara gave a howl of triumph and punched the air. Sky let go of Moonflight's reins and climbed stiffly away, then came swooping down again from the cliff top, talons extended to pick up his rider.

Cara signaled to Ronan, and they held Breena between them, at arm's length. "Sky!" Cara's voice was almost gone. She tried again. "Sky! Take Breena first. Breena! She needs help."

Again, Cara was unsure whether Sky would understand her, much less obey—but the dragon dutifully wrapped his talons around Breena's shoulders, taking care not to hurt her, and lifted her into the night sky.

Ronan took hold of Cara, supporting her against the buffeting waves. "Are you all right?"

"Yes—Ronan, how can I thank you . . . ?"

"Some other time. I must go back to Mordannsair—he will be worried. Come and see me, after the storm."

"After the storm," echoed Cara. "I will!"

Then she felt the grip of Sky's talons, the suction as the sea's hold was broken, the sudden rush of cold air—and all the energy that had kept her going through the long hours of searching and the perils of the rescue seemed to flood out of her, leaving her limp, weak, and exhausted.

Sky set her down gently on the grass at the cliff top, and settled to the ground a short distance away. His chest rose and fell as he took in great gulps of air. His wings were quivering, and he held them half extended, as though it was too painful to fold them completely. Poor, brave Sky! Cara made to go and comfort him.

But then a terrible keening stopped her in her tracks. She turned to see Moonflight, shuffling on her belly, nuzzle a still form that lay on the ground amid a half circle of guard flight riders and their dragons. Cara stumbled toward them.

Breena lay on her back, her wet hair plastered across her face. Moonflight's cries and nudges were unavailing. Breena did not move. She did not seem to be breathing.

Rain began to fall. Around the melancholy scene, the unearthly wailing of the Cave of Sighs rose above the howling of the wind.

RECONCILIATIONS

Cara sat by Breena's bedside in the infirmary at South Landing.

Besides the chair on which she was sitting, the room contained an iron bed with white sheets as creaseless as newly fallen snow and a wooden bedside cabinet. The window was tall and narrow, with small panes of glass. There was a vase on the windowsill with a bunch of wildflowers in it. Cara had picked them. Breena was lying in bed, propped up on pillows so overstuffed that she seemed to be resting against a pile of clouds, looking as pale and delicate as a china doll. She had been asleep when Cara had arrived, and Cara had not wanted to wake her.

Breena stirred. She blinked sleepily at Cara.

"Hello," said Cara awkwardly.

Breena's eyes widened. She tried to smile, and then to say something, but her voice wouldn't come. She closed her eyes. Fat tears rolled down her cheeks.

Cara put her arms around her until her sobs died away.

"I'm sorry," said Breena in a small voice.

Cara pulled away and looked her in the eyes. "No. I'm the one who should be sorry. I forgot what really matters."

Breena said, "I forgot, too."

There was the sort of awkward pause that happens when two people have so many things to say that they can't find a place to begin.

To break the silence, Cara said, "We thought we'd lost you for a moment there, on the cliff top, and then you went down with a fever. How are you feeling now?"

Breena stared at her for a moment. Then she gave a snort of laughter. "What kind of silly question is that to be asking someone in my condition?" She giggled, and then clutched at her ribs. "Oh, don't make me laugh, it hurts. If you want the truth, I feel like something the wyvern's had."

"Well, the surgeons say you're doing very well," Cara told her. "That's why they let me in to see you today. They wouldn't allow any visitors last week except your ma and da."

"Don't I know it," said Breena. "Every time I woke up, there was Ma crying and Da wagging his finger, saying he always knew that something terrible would happen to me, mucking around with dragons and not sticking to fish! I didn't have the strength to remind them that it was the sea that nearly did me in, in the end!" She suddenly fell silent. In a much more subdued voice, she went on, "I never had the chance to thank you. . . ."

Cara shook her head. "There's no need."

"There is, though." Breena took Cara's hand. "I thought I was going to die, Cara. I really did. Me and Moony. And all I could think of was how I wished I'd made up with you before. . . ." Her voice faltered.

"I was thinking the same thing." Cara's throat felt as if she were wearing a collar three sizes too tight. "All the time I was looking for you, I was thinking, *I just want to find Breena, and know she's all right, and have the chance to say I'm sorry*. . . ." She shook her head. "I've been an awful fool."

"Well," said Breena quietly, "I've been a bigger one."

Cara tried to laugh. "Let's not start a competition." Breena gave her an uncertain smile, and Cara went on. "Let's see, what can I tell you? My da has moved Sky and Moony down to a farm on the Walds—"

"Are they all right?" Breena asked quickly.

"In good shape, considering," said Cara briskly. "Da's renting a barn," she went on. "There was no way of getting Sky and Moony back to Dragonsdale, and Alberich wanted them away from the cliff top as soon as possible, with Leaf-fall coming on. He's been over to see them every day, and Drane has moved in with them. He's set up a camp bed in one of the mangers, and he's been up all hours applying poultices, changing dressings, and making sure that Moony takes her medicine."

Breena looked concerned. "Medicine?"

"Oh, don't worry," Cara told her hurriedly, "it's just a bit of a cough. Probably from all that time in the water. Drane's on top of it. He's got a real talent for looking after sick dragons—and to think I used to think he was useless!" Cara gave a shamefaced chuckle.

"Anyway, Moony's wing is knitting well and her sails are mending. She's as tough as they come—just like her rider."

Breena groaned. "I don't feel very tough at the moment."

"Not to worry—Gerda sent something along to build up your strength." Cara went to the foot of the bed. With the air of a conjurer, she produced from the floor a large wicker basket, full to the brim with cakes, pies, and fruits of every description.

Breena eyed the basket. "Build up my strength? How am I supposed to do that? By lifting it?"

"I think you're supposed to eat it."

"How long does Gerda expect me to be here? There's enough there to feed the whole infirmary!"

"Wony did the packing, and she insisted on putting in as much as possible—especially cake! She sends her love and best wishes."

"Wony." Breena nodded. "Will you say thank you from me, for what she did? It was very brave of her, going back to Dragonsdale all alone to get help."

"You can tell her yourself," said Cara. "She's coming to visit you tomorrow. So's Drane, if he can tear himself away from his patients—" She broke off. Breena was staring out the window, her eyes wet with tears.

"Why did we let it happen, Cara?"

In a low voice, Cara said, "I got so wrapped up in myself, I forgot to think about other people."

"I was just jealous—like a little kid who sees that someone else has a bigger lollipop. And I was fool enough to listen to Hortense."

"So was I," said Cara meekly. She took Breena's hand.

After a while, Breena said, "I've been thinking I might leave Dragonsdale."

"What?" Cara gaped at her friend. "Why?"

"I'm not sure I should be riding anymore. After all the accidents I've had . . ."

"Don't be silly," said Cara. "You know what Mistress Hildebrand says: 'If you fall off a dragon, you must get back on straightaway.' As soon as you get back on Moony, you'll be fine, I know you will."

Breena shook her head. "I'm not scared for myself, I'm scared for Moony. I don't want to lose her, and I've put her at risk too many times. And I don't think she'll trust me anymore. There's no reason I can think of why she should."

"That's not true!" cried Cara. "After what you two have been through, your Trustbond will be even stronger!"

Breena shook her head. "Anyway, I'm just not a good enough rider—that's why Galen won't have me in the guard flight. I don't deserve a dragon like Moony. I don't deserve to ride any dragon, ever again."

"Now I know you're delirious!" Cara told her. "How could you even think of living without dragons? Some of that seawater must have gotten into your brain. Look,

I didn't tell you this, but Moonflight is pining for you. She's off her food, and every time I show up, she comes bounding up to see who it is, and when she realizes it's only me, she slinks back to her stable and mopes."

Breena picked at the hem on her top sheet and said nothing. Cara's mind was in a whirl. How could she remind Breena of all that dragons gave their riders? The way they moved—heavy, lumbering beasts on the ground, but light, graceful, powerful creatures in the air. The way they lifted you up into the freedom of the skies, took you away from the dullness of the everyday; the way they responded to the lightest touch of your hands or legs. Yet all the time you knew the unpredictability of these great creatures, that at any second the dragon could be rid of you with a flick of its great muscled body.

And what about the hours spent caring for them? Feeding, cleaning out, grooming, tending to them when they were ill, and above all . . . loving them. How could Cara say all this? She didn't have the words—and anyway, Breena surely knew it, too. There must be another reason. . . .

"Why do you really want to go away? Is it because of me?"

"No!" Breena turned away. "I just can't face it, Cara." Her voice was barely above a whisper. "I can't face going back—knowing that everyone's laughing at me."

"Now, stop that! Nobody's laughing. Everybody's missing you. If they didn't care for you, why did the entire stable turn out to search for three days in terrible weather?"

"I know!" cried Breena. "And how can I ever repay them? How can I ever repay you?"

"By getting well," Cara told her, "and coming back to us and getting back on Moony and riding her."

Breena sighed. "Well . . . I'll think about it. And I'll do my best to get fit in the next three weeks, so I can come and watch you win the Island Championships."

Cara shook her head. "I'm not going to the championships."

Breena stared at her. "Not going? Why not? You're the best rider in Seahaven, and Sky's the best dragon. . . ."

"He's not going to be fit," said Cara gently. "His flight muscles are badly strained from the accident at the showing and then pulling Moony up the cliff. Alberich has forbidden me to ride him for six weeks. And so has Da," she added.

Breena was distraught. "Oh, no, Cara! It's all my fault! I'm so, so sorry."

"I'm not. You know how I said I forgot what's important? When you and Moony went missing, I remembered. 'Friends matter more than rosettes.' Hortense said that."

Breena stared. "I never thought I'd hear you agreeing with Hortense."

"She was right, though." Cara gave a rueful smile. "The sad thing—the really sad thing, for Hortense—is that although she said it, she doesn't believe it. But I do."

"And so do I." Breena reached out for Cara's hand and held it.

"Ahem!"

With a start, Cara and Breena turned toward the door. Galen was standing there. The leader of the guard flight was a big man, but could be disconcertingly quiet—he was a hunter, after all. He had entered the room without either Breena or Cara noticing.

"How's the patient faring?" he asked.

Breena reddened and tried to sit up, wincing as a spasm of pain pulsed down her arm.

"Rest easy, Breena." Galen held up a hand and stepped forward. "How's the arm?"

"Still sore, but not broken," replied Breena sheepishly. "Thank you."

"And I hear from Drane that Moonflight's injuries are mending apace." Galen sat down on the edge of the bed, which creaked in response to his weight. "Well, you've the look of a plucked moorcock about you, and for good reason. Still, rest and good eating will take care of that." He indicated the basket of food. "And I see you're not likely to go hungry." He cleared his throat and said awkwardly, "Now, about the guard flight . . ."

"It's all right, Galen." Breena's voice was calm. "I've messed up too often, I know that. I know you won't want me in the guard flight. I shan't pester you anymore."

"Well, see it from my point of view," said Galen. "A rider who goes hunting when she's no business to, and then injures her dragon? A rider who's had a terrible season, who's been caught up in a midair collision and then got herself lost? A rider who's not won a Junior Championship?" Galen shook his grizzled head. "No, that's not a rider I'd want in my wing."

Cara glared at the old warrior, hating him. How could he torment Breena like this? For her part, Breena just looked straight at Galen, dry-eyed, saying nothing.

"But then again," Galen went on in the same quiet, measured tones, "a rider who survives three days on a beach with nothing to eat but pebbles; a rider who tends her injured dragon with nothing more than kindness and seaweed, who could save herself but refuses to abandon her dragon; a rider who refuses to give in to fear when she's nearly getting drowned twice a day and everything seems lost; a rider who insists that her dragon is rescued before herself—and, incidentally, a rider who Mistress Hildebrand says is one of the best she's ever trained . . . well, that's exactly the sort of rider I need in the guard flight."

He stood up. "Alberich says he expects Moonflight to be fit to fly by the end of Leaf-fall, so make sure you're ready by then. No malingering, mind! I shall expect you for training at dawn on the First of Mistide. What say you, then?"

Breena abruptly turned over and buried her face in her pillow. Her shoulders shook.

Cara, her eyes shining, turned to Galen. "She says yes."

FRIENDS OLD
AND NEW

The last days of Leaf-fall were crisp and bright—just perfect for riding out. As far as Breena and Cara were concerned, this was a sad waste: Breena's convalescence had been slow and she was still not allowed to fly, and Cara would go nowhere without Breena.

But at long last, after solemn discussion, Alberich, Gerda, Huw, and Mistress Hildebrand had agreed that Breena was fit to ride. And so, early one morning, Cara and Breena tacked up the now fully recovered Skydancer and Moonflight and, along with Wony and Bumble, flew out to Merfolk Bay. Even Drane had been persuaded to join the girls on their ride, his desire to meet Ronan having overcome his dread of flying. Even so, he spent the journey clinging to the saddle behind Cara, whimpering occasionally and keeping his eyes tightly shut.

They crossed the dark hills and barren moors. They swooped over a forest of oak and beech whose autumn leaves, torn from twig and branch by the wind of their passing, spiraled briefly behind them before falling to earth in showers of brown and golden rain. Then the wide expanse of the sea was in sight, and they turned in to land on the shore of Merfolk Bay.

At Cara's bidding, Sky slapped his tail on the water to summon Ronan. Waves lapped peacefully at the shore as the companions stood on the rocks, waiting for the merboy to answer their call.

Cara gazed out across the bay: at the blue sky, the wispy clouds, the placid blue-gray sea. "A lot's happened since we went to Spindrift Cove," she said.

Breena gave up trying to coax Moonflight closer to the waves and came to stand at her friend's shoulder. "Just a bit," she said wryly. "Hasn't it, Moony?" The dragon snorted, nodded, and took another step back from the water's edge.

Some distance from the shore, the horned heads of a flock of capricorns appeared. In their midst, there was a sudden explosion of spray as the graceful form of Mordannsair leapt from the sea. Cara beamed at the appearance of the sea-dragon, Breena and Drane gasped, and Wony cried out in wonder.

At the height of Mordannsair's leap, Ronan threw himself clear of his plunging mount and dived into the sea. Moments later, Mordannsair reappeared among the capricorns and Ronan resurfaced a dragonlength from the rocks.

"Ronan!" cried Cara, overjoyed that he had answered Sky's call so quickly.

"Cara!" The merboy seemed equally delighted to see his human friend. "I had expected to see you before this."

"I'm sorry." Cara held out her hand to help Ronan onto the rocks. "Sky couldn't fly for a long time, and then Breena couldn't, and she wanted to come and say thank you."

Breena was staring at the merboy in undisguised wonder. "That's right," she said. "It wasn't much of a conversation we had the last time we met."

"I am glad I was able to help," said Ronan, "and I am sorry I startled you when I first appeared."

"Startled?" Breena laughed. "You nearly scared the life out of me!"

Ronan looked concerned. "I am sorry to have added to your troubles."

"Don't be!" Breena told him warmly. "Without you, I wouldn't be here now, nor would Moony. Thank you." She held out her hand and Ronan shook it.

"This is Drane," Cara said, remembering her manners and ushering her gaping friend forward. "And you've already met Wony. She brought the guard flight to rescue Breena and Moony."

Ronan solemnly shook hands with each of them in turn. "I am glad you were able to bring help in time," he told Wony. "You were very brave to fly in such a storm."

Wony turned crimson with pleasure. She had just begun to say, "It was Bumble, really . . ." when a flight of four dragons appeared over the cliffs, heading for the bay and Ronan's flock of capricorns. Even from the ground, Cara could make out the familiar riding colors. She clenched her fists.

"Hortense!" she snapped. "Has she dared to come here again?"

Ronan nodded tersely. "Several times since you were here last."

"We'll see about that. Breena, Wony, quickly!" Cara ran to Sky. Within seconds she was airborne, with Breena and Wony in close attendance.

The confrontation with Hortense's friends was brief. Their dragons, evidently remembering their last encounter with the Goldenbrow, shied away from Sky instantly. Only furious shrieks and frantic cuts from their riders' whips persuaded them not to turn tail and fly for safety.

That left Ernestina and Hortense herself. Cara signaled to them to land. With a smirk that made Cara's fingers twitch, Hortense signed agreement and led her companions to touch down on the rocks where Drane and Ronan were waiting.

Hortense stared at her opponents with disdain, pointedly ignoring Ronan. In her most languid voice, she drawled, "Cara, this is becoming such a bore. You're stopping us from enjoying ourselves."

"Enjoying yourselves?!" Cara was disgusted. Ronan thrashed angrily at the water with his tail.

"We just want to hunt these wild creatures and you're hindering us once again. Just wait until I tell my father."

"I don't care about your father, and the capricorns belong to Ronan."

"Really?" Hortense sounded incredulous. "Have they been branded? Is there a certificate of ownership? Or a bill of sale?"

Cara said nothing.

"I thought not." Hortense turned to her hangers-on with a triumphant sneer. "Tell her what my father says about hunting."

"Lord Torin says all creatures of the sea can be hunted," said hanger-on number one.

"That's right," confirmed hanger-on number two. "Because they are wild and don't belong to anyone."

Hortense stared Cara hard in the face. "My father makes the rules. He says the goat-fish can be hunted. They don't belong to anyone or anything."

"They are mine!" cried Ronan.

"It speaks!" Hortense stared at the merboy and raised her eyebrows in mock surprise. "So this is Cara's fish-tailed boyfriend!"

"He has a name." Cara stepped forward with her fists balled. "And he isn't my boyfriend." She stopped and fell silent, then threw back her head and laughed.

"Oh, Hortense, you really are priceless."

Hortense regarded her with suspicion. "What?"

"The way you dig and worm and get under people's skin—it's a gift, I suppose. I'm just glad it's one I don't have. The trouble is, it only works once." Cara drew Breena to her side, and the two girls stood arm in arm. "You turned us against each other—but you won't do it again. Right, Breena?"

Breena nodded grimly. "Right."

"That goes for me, too," said Wony stoutly. Drane nodded.

"You're wasting your time here," Cara told Hortense. "None of us will take any notice of what you say, ever again."

Hortense's face was livid with anger. "Do you really think that I'm in any way concerned about what you think, do, or say? I am the High Lord's daughter!" She pointed her riding whip at Cara. "You think you're so clever, you and your oh-isn't-he-so-wonderful dragon." Skydancer gave a screech of defiance and took off.

"That's right," shrieked Hortense triumphantly, "fly away, you overgrown wyvern! And as for the rest of you . . . you're just a rabble of pathetic nothings." Hortense was so taken up with her outburst of spite that she completely failed to notice the dark shadow that had begun to envelop her, growing larger and larger. She pointed at Drane, Breena, and Wony in turn. "You, you're nothing but a glorified swineherd,

you're a
complete failure as a
rider, you're a silly little beginner—
fools and wastrels, the lot of you—" A crack of mighty
wings drowned her words. She looked up and screamed
as Skydancer swooped down, talons outstretched.

"No, Sky!" cried Cara.

But Skydancer ignored her command. His talons
clasped Hortense's shoulders and he plucked her from
the ground.

Hortense gave a howl of terror. "Put me down!"

But Skydancer did no such thing. With easy wing beats, he headed out toward the sea, carrying his struggling captive.

"What's he doing?" hissed Breena.

"I wish I knew." Cara's heart was in her mouth. What was Sky up to? Was he remembering the time last year when he had dunked Hortense in the Dragonsmere? Did he have some kind of a plan? With Sky, it was hard to tell.

The hangers-on wailed. Ernestina watched with detached interest.

Skydancer turned and flew lower. Hortense's feet dipped into the sea, sending up two plumes of water. Drane grinned.

A short way from the shore, Sky dipped down and released his grip. Hortense flopped into the water, right in the middle of the flock of capricorns.

"He's dropped her!" Wony blinked. "Why has he done that?"

Her question was answered as the capricorns circled in toward the place where Hortense was thrashing about.

Drane said, "I think they want to play."

Ronan gave Cara a concerned look. "Should I call them off?"

Cara's smile would have terrified a shark. "Not yet," she said.

The capricorns were getting bolder. One by one, they spiraled in and butted Hortense with their hard little horns. Cara knew what those horns could do—one blow from them had knocked her down even though the capricorn had been in a rock pool with barely enough water to swim in. Out in the sea, the buttings they were giving Hortense would be formidable indeed.

From the noise she was making, Hortense obviously thought so. "Ow!" she screeched. "Ooh! Oof! Get them off me!"

Her cries became increasingly frantic as more and more capricorns joined in the game. One rose up from beneath Hortense to send her howling a quarter dragonlength into the air. As she came down, the flock closed in, butting Hortense unmercifully, flicking her from head to head like a bunch of stable hands playing keep-away with an inflated pig's bladder.

Hortense's two hangers-on scrambled down from their dragons and threw stones and handfuls of seaweed at the capricorns, but they were much too far away for their missiles to reach. "Leave her alone!" they cried. "Go away, you nasty things!"

Ernestina remained in her saddle. Cara detected the trace of a smile as she watched the High Lord's daughter being flung around like a rag doll.

Hortense's shrill cries were increasing in noise and frequency. "Do something!" Her screams were abruptly cut off as a capricorn butted her in the stomach.

Ronan turned to Cara and Breena. "Whatever she has done in the past, I do not wish harm to come to her."

"Wait," said Cara. "I've got an idea." She strode to the water's edge and cupped her hands around her mouth. "Did you say, 'Call them off'?"

"Yes, of course I—urghhh!" Hortense's head dipped beneath the water. Surfacing, she cried, "Tell the fish-boy to get them off me!"

"How can he do that," replied Cara, "if they're wild animals?"

"I don't know—I don't care—tell him to call them off!"

"He can't, if they're wild. But"—Cara went on as though the idea had just occurred to her—"if he calls them off, and they obey him—well, that would prove that they belong to him, wouldn't it?"

"Why, you . . ." Hortense howled as another set of capricorn horns found its mark.

"Wouldn't it?"

"Yes, yes," yelled Hortense. "Anything you say!"

"And if they belong to Ronan, that proves they aren't wild animals, doesn't it?"

"Yes! Ow! All right, I agree!"

"And you promise that you and your friends won't hunt them anymore?"

"I promise! Just get them off me!"

Cara nodded at Ronan. "You can call them off now."

Ronan slapped his tail against the water in a series of beats. Mordannsair burst from the sea and swam toward the capricorns, who instantly broke off their attack and dived beneath the waves. Ronan slipped from the rocks and helped Hortense to shore. She was weeping with fury, and more frightened than hurt. The capricorns had been less rough with her than her reactions had suggested — or than she deserved, thought Cara.

Bruised and bedraggled, with strands of seaweed hanging from her hair, Hortense was hauled from the water by her friends. Drane, Wony, Cara, and Breena looked on, grinning broadly.

Once she was safe on land, Hortense shook off her twittering followers and turned on Cara and her friends. "That was a deliberate attempt to drown me! I'm going to tell my father about this!"

"You do that, Hortense," said Breena calmly. "And while you're at it, don't forget to tell him about your promise."

"You haven't heard the last of this! I'll get you all back!" Sobbing with vexation, Hortense scrambled into her saddle and lashed out with her whip. Her startled dragon took to the air. With plaintive cries of "Wait for us!" the two hangers-on followed.

Hortense circled overhead once, inviting Ernestina to join her. When Ernestina made no move, the High Lord's daughter turned her dragon's head toward her father's manor and flew away.

Only then did Ernestina turn to Cara. "I owe you an apology."

Cara stared at her. "Do you? Why?"

"When Hortense tricked you into flying badly at Clapperclaw, she did it so that I could win."

Breena stepped forward indignantly, but Cara motioned to her to be quiet.

"I didn't know what she was planning," continued Ernestina, "and I'd have stopped her if I could. But I still feel bad about it."

Breena could no longer keep silent. "Too late for that," she said. "You didn't feel so bad that it stopped you from going on and winning the Junior Championship."

"And you wouldn't have, if Cara had been flying," said Wony. Drane nodded agreement.

Ernestina shrugged. "We'll just have to wait until next season to find out, won't we? One thing I will promise you," she went on. "I'll make sure that Hortense's oath is known at Clapperclaw. No more hunting of capricorns, you can be sure of that."

Cara nodded. "I'll see you in the show ring next season."

"I'll look forward to it." Ernestina touched her hat to Cara.

"Ernestina—wait!" Cara took hold of Ernestina's stirrup iron. "You and Hortense—how can you stomach her?"

In a deliberately unconcerned voice, Ernestina said, "We're not all lucky enough to have a father who is High Lord—or a Dragonmaster."

She flicked her reins. Stormbringer leapt into the sky and headed back toward Clapperclaw, leaving a startled silence behind her.

At length, Cara shook herself. The sun was already sinking below the horizon. "We should be getting back."

"Not just yet." Breena held out a hand to Ronan. Surprised, he took it. Breena motioned Cara to take Ronan's other hand, and they joined hands with Drane and Wony to complete a circle.

Once this was done, Breena intoned an old Bresalian oath of friendship.

> *"The Peace of the running wave to you,*
> *The Peace of the flowing air to you . . ."*

The others joined in the oath and the solemn, joyous words rang out over the lapping waves.

> *"Friends we be from the starting,*
> *Friends forever, never parting . . .*
> *Friends we are and friends we be,*
> *Friends for all eternity."*

Out in the bay, Skydancer splashed down among the excited capricorns, who immediately began a game of chase-the-dragon's-tail. Mordannsair approached Sky cautiously. Sky-dragon and sea-dragon stretched out toward each other and rubbed noses.

Cara smiled. Jealousy and suspicion were powerful in their way. They could tear people apart. But goodwill and kindness were more powerful still. More lasting. Stronger than the storm.

Fire and water could be friends after all.

AN EXCERPT FROM

DRAGON CARE

THE OFFICIAL MANUAL OF THE
BRESALIAN DRAGON SOCIETY

REPRINTED BY PERMISSION

CHAPTER 2
CARING FOR YOUR DRAGON

Like humans, dragons differ from each other; they each have their own personalities and so cannot all be treated the same.

In order to develop a successful Trustbond, a dragonrider must forge a relationship with her or his dragon and be observant, sympathetic, and understanding. By spending time with and studying her or his dragon, a dragonrider will come to know the personality of a dragon and the dragon will come to know the dragonrider.

GROOMING

Grooming is an important part of developing the Trustbond. Daily physical contact and care for the dragon will help to create an intimacy between rider and dragon.

Grooming should be undertaken before and after exercise. Thoroughness is important.

HOW TO GROOM

Gather together your grooming kit; all of your supplies should be kept together for ease and tidiness. Talk softly to your dragon from a distance as you approach it—you don't want to scare it and cause an involuntary flaming!

- Beginning at the head, wash all mud and dust from the dragon with a cloth and soapy water.
- Pick out all mud and dirt between scales with a scale scraper (FIG. 1). Run your fingertips between the scales to make sure all dirt has been removed.
- Begin to polish the dragon's body with buffer brushes (FIGS. 2–4). Use a lower-numbered brush for younger dragons, since their scales are not as hard as an older dragon's.
- Work slowly all down the body, taking care when brushing near the tender parts of the dragon.
- Using the clawpicker (FIG. 5), pick out all dirt between and in the claws.
- Polish the scales with a clean, dry cloth (FIG. 6) and scale polish (FIG. 7).
- Continue on to the sails (make sure that there is plenty of room for your dragon to extend its wings, so that all of the sail is exposed). Using sail oil (FIG. 8) and a clean, dry cloth, oil the dragon's sails from the front of the wing to the trailing edge.
- Finally, apply claw wax (FIG. 9) to the claws and polish to a shine with a lint cloth.

For claw clipping (FIG. 10), *teeth filing* (FIG. 11), *and scale growth* (FIG. 12), *see* Chapter 4: **Dragon Health**.

FIG. 1
Scale scraper
(for cleaning between scales)

GROOMING KIT

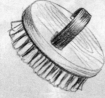

FIGS. 2–4
Buffing brushes, various types
(for polishing scales)

No. 1 buffer

No. 2 buffer

No. 3 buffer

FIG. 5
Clawpicker
(for cleaning claws)

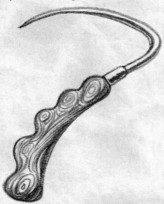

FIG. 6
Polishing cloth

FIG. 7
Scale polish

Doctor Oakapple's famous scale polish

FIG. 8
Sail oil

Sail Oil

FIG. 9
Claw wax

CLAW WAX

FIG. 10
Claw trimmer

FIG. 11
Tooth file
(for maintaining the dragon's teeth and, therefore, firing ability)

FIG. 12
Scale rasp
(for filing off growth on the scales)

SALAMANDA DRAKE

Salamanda Drake is sixteen years old and lives with her father, a dragon-trader, on the Isles of Bresal.

Her love of dragons began at the age of three, when her da began taking her to fairs and showings around the islands. Discovering she had a special way with even the most unruly of creatures, she soon learned that (in her own words) "the only way to train a dragon is to be patient and never give up."

Salamanda spends much of her free time—sometimes when she should be at school!—sweeping, grooming, and exercising her father's dragons. Salamanda has a Trustbond with Hillsweeper, a Firecrest dragon, and together they are now competing at showings. They have high hopes of representing Finnglass at the Island Championships.

Salamanda's other great love is writing. She discovered her talent following a serious riding accident at the age of thirteen.

Translated from the original Bresal edition, *Riding the Storm* is Salamanda's second story in a planned series about the dragonriders of Bresal.